SHERLOCK HOLMES' LOST ADVENTURE

SHERLOCK HOLMES' LOST ADVENTURE

The True Story of the Giant Rats of Sumatra

Lauren Steinhauer

iUniverse, Inc.
New York Lincoln Shanghai

Sherlock Holmes' Lost Adventure
The True Story of the Giant Rats of Sumatra

All Rights Reserved © 2004 by Lauren Steinhauer

No part of this book may be reproduced or transmitted in any form or by any means, graphic, electronic, or mechanical, including photocopying, recording, taping, or by any information storage retrieval system, without the written permission of the publisher.

iUniverse, Inc.

For information address:
iUniverse, Inc.
2021 Pine Lake Road, Suite 100
Lincoln, NE 68512
www.iuniverse.com

ISBN: 0-595-31707-3 (pbk)
ISBN: 0-595-66386-9 (cloth)

Printed in the United States of America

To "Captain" Al Paulsen and his Alice Fair, to my big brother and ace private eye, René, for his tireless help with my manuscript, to my younger brother, Ron, for returning to the fold, to Dr. Milin for all his insights, to Mother and Father at rest in Heaven, to sweet Mother in Zamboanga and especially to Eskimo for only *everything*.

Contents

Chapter 1	An Early Morning's Case	1
Chapter 2	A Mystery Unfolds	9
Chapter 3	The Lady Vanishes	13
Chapter 4	The Metaphysician	19
Chapter 5	The Mendicant Friar	29
Chapter 6	Theft at the Monastery	37
Chapter 7	A Holiday Cut Short	41
Chapter 8	A Lady in Distress	45
Chapter 9	Catherine de Quincey	51
Chapter 10	A Plot Thickens	55
Chapter 11	The Meddler	61
Chapter 12	Down House	65
Chapter 13	The Great Man's Dilemma	71
Chapter 14	Tommy	79
Chapter 15	An Unexpected Visitor	89
Chapter 16	Mrs. Hudson's Account	93
Chapter 17	An Identity Revealed	99
Chapter 18	Sumatra Calls	103
Chapter 19	The Gates of Hell	111
Chapter 20	Return to Baker Street	121
Chapter 21	A Grave Message	125
Chapter 22	Lofcadio Hearseborne III	129

Chapter 23	The Akashic Record	137
Chapter 24	The Giant Rats of Sumatra	149
Chapter 25	The Return Home	159
Chapter 26	A View to a Life	161
Chapter 27	The Conclusion	165

About the Author 169

CHAPTER 1

An Early Morning's Case

In a life marked by good fortune—earning my medical degree from the University of London, serving with the 5th Regiment of Foot in Afghanistan—I count among my supreme blessings the opportunity early on in my friendship with Mr. Sherlock Holmes to accompany him *en train* across the continent. Observing occurrences firsthand I should otherwise have found beyond my belief, I came to serve as the instrument of immortalizing the great detective's exploits, as I had for Holmes' first case of significance; that adventure I published as *A Study in Scarlet* six years after the fact.

Then there was the vile habit to which Holmes turned whenever matters went counter to his desires. As each day passed barren of the next memorable case, his dependence on the needle would grow along with my lingering concern for his welfare. I trusted that the trip to which I have alluded would distract his thoughts from any pharmacological inclinations.

So it was one fine morning in the year 1882 that I returned home from my constitutional. I ascended the steps within the Baker Street lodgings I shared with my singular friend when I encountered a portly, middle-aged woman painfully making her way down the staircase, tears streaming from reddened eyes, a sopping-wet kerchief draped around rotund fingers like uncooked sausages.

By necessity I descended backwards, careful footstep by footstep, whilst I declared, "Dear lady, I am Dr. Watson. May I be of assistance?"

"It's Mr. Sherlock Holmes," she blubbered as we reached the base of the stairs together. "He has no time for me nor my little Laura."

"Laura?" I repeated.

"My little girl, sir, my Laura. She disappeared on an errand last night. She's a good little girl, always does as she's told. Come nightfall, she hadn't shown herself. By then I was worried sick, worried enough to find the costermonger to ask if my daughter ever stopped by for me. He said that she was there, rather late like. I asked him if he was sure who my Laura was, and he said he knew her right well, that he took note of her visits for her bright chatter and the little whittled wooden doll Laura always carries about.

"Here it is now, Doctor, a night and a morning after, and still no sign of my angel. And no help from Mr. Holmes, sir, no help t'all."

I had come to learn that Holmes' reaction to such entreaties was wildly unpredictable. At times, he would rally to the aid of a member of the powerless and of the dispossessed. On these occasions he betrayed a deep-seated compassion for the underdog better suited to our brethren across the Atlantic. Alas, more often than not he displayed a chilling indifference to the plight or social station of the supplicant. Holmes so vacillated between these two states, I often imagined he carried a magical die to cast at such times, allowing the randomness of the toss to dictate his sentiment for the moment.

"And how came you to grace us with your problem, dear lady?" I asked.

"A gentleman I know, sir, with a dear, little dog. He tells me Mr. Holmes is a wonder with all manner of puzzles and the like. And with a heart of gold. Big as the channel, he says."

"Ah, you live in Lambeth, then," I remarked, "by Mr. Sherman."

"Right, sir, but how on earth—?"

"Ah, well, dear lady, it is a skill called deduction, takes years to master."

"Well, however you did it, you're right as rain, sir. We live near where the gentleman runs his trade. Mr. Holmes and him and his dog, Toby, I think is the name, work together, my friend says, at unraveling all sorts of dark goin's-on, and he puts great strength in Mr. Holmes finding my little Laura." With the soiled kerchief, the woman delicately dabbed at the corners of her eyes. "But Mr. Holmes, he takes no notice of me, sir."

"Can you furnish me with a description?"

"Of my Laura? Oh, the face of an angel, Doctor! Long yellow hair like corn silk, blue eyes, three foot tall or there abouts. I tell you straight away, I'm poor. I've no money, but I'll raise it. And hell along with it. Anything to see my little Laura back home safe. I'm beggin' you. Help a lonely old woman find her little girl." The woman burst into tears, her legs giving beneath her. On bent knees, she grasped at my trousers and cried, "Help me! For God's sake, help me! My Laura, my poor Laura!"

"Dear lady," I declared, fumbling to release her hold on my pant legs and with some effort assisting her to her feet, "Holmes is simply preoccupied. I shall talk to him. I shall convince him. I assure you, he shall find your little Laura." As she gushed forth a profusion of "thank you's," I had her scribble her name and address on a notepad, then reasserted on our way to the door that I would do all in my power to have Holmes locate her child.

Finally, I approached the sitting-room upstairs only to hear a lilting voice issuing past the door. On entering, I beheld the radiant face of a young woman. In that instance I knew the searing power of lightning coursing through one's body; my legs buckled under my weight; my heart beat savagely in my chest, so powerful the emotion flooding my being. Never had I felt such incandescent passion. I struggled to regain my composure whilst Holmes, unaware of my state, peered through one of the windows facing Baker Street.

The young woman seemed fragile and diminutive, as of the finest bone china, and as she spoke her eyes radiated flickering bolts of the most intense cornflower blue. She was modestly but impeccably appointed, white-gloved, a choker of finest silk hugging her swan-like neck. I recall thinking to myself in most uncharacteristic fashion: Oh, to be one thread of that shimmering cloth!

I became aware of Holmes just saying, "Am I to understand you ask Sherlock Holmes to believe that your man servant was murdered for the theft of a mere typewriting machine?"

Still in a fog, I watched her faultless lips forming the words, "The typewriter was of some value, sir."

Steadying my nerves, I cleared my throat and with trepidation directed a question to the young woman.

"A gift from a friend?"

Turning round, Holmes shot a disapproving glare my way. With knitted brow, he cocked his head in that manner of his that made one feel infinitely exposed as the subtlest demeanor of the body fell under his scrutiny.

I moved a few paces nearer the vision before me, and my legs turned once more to aspic. She gently shook the hand that I offered, gave me the slightest of smiles and answered, "No, sir, the machine was left to me by a dear relative, an uncle."

With relief I eagerly volunteered, "Dr. John Watson," though my voice quivered, and I smiled too broadly in retrospect. "At your service."

Was it my imagination, or had I been favoured with a blush upon the young woman's cheeks?

"Who should wish, I wonder, to commit murder for so small a prize as a typewriting machine, Miss…"

"Gates. Lucy Gates, Doctor."

All this while, my profound interest in the young woman's dilemma seemed to puzzle Holmes. I had observed first-hand my friend's inestimable powers of observation concerning matters nefarious. But in matters of the heart I discovered soon after meeting him that he was hopelessly perplexed by man's baser drives and all the more by the rarified mysteries of the heart.

"If you please, Watson," he testily interjected.

Holmes' attention turned back to Lucy Gates.

"I ask you again, young lady, what other items were stolen?"

"My answer remains the same, sir. None." Her spirited response did little to lessen my admiration for her.

To my annoyance, Holmes persisted, "You mean to imply no other items of value rest in your household?"

"I imply nothing of the sort, Mr. Holmes. I own a modest collection of Bavarian crystal, some silver, jewelry of limited value."

"And the other missing items?" Holmes brusquely pressed.

"Holmes," I interceded, "the young lady has answered you!"

"Nothing, save a typewriting machine?" he continued.

"Yes, sir." For the first time I heard a quaver in her otherwise melodious voice.

"Posh," Holmes countered. "If a client be not candid with me, I can offer no assistance."

"Holmes," I protested, uneasy to find myself in alliance with this beautiful stranger and in opposition to Holmes, "can you not tell that the young lady is being candid with you?"

"Is she?" Holmes pointedly questioned.

"Nevertheless, Miss Gates," he declared, "I am occupied. I direct you to any number of other investigative services in the City of London."

A disheartened look appeared upon the young woman's features, and her gaze fixed upon her gloved hands.

"Then there is no more to be said, Mr. Holmes?" she weakly pressed, a plaintive glance in my direction.

"Nothing."

Lucy Gates gathered the folds of her dress and stiffly rose, a tear welling in her eye, and silently brushed past me. I froze when she paused at the door, turned to direct a last glimpse at me, then glided down the stairs. Instinctively, I took a step in her direction, so moved was I by whatever situation had compelled her to approach the stern presence of my friend.

I leapt to the window in hope of catching a glimpse of Lucy Gates on the street below. As luck had it, she was just slipping a comely foot into a brougham. The cab pulled swiftly away into the bustling street, but I caught the number 195; I knew I would remember it forever. My heart began to sink with despair that I might never lay eyes upon the young woman again. She was everything in womanhood of which I had ever dreamt: The comely shape of her face, the sparkle in her eyes, how her flaxen hair fell and framed her loveliness. In the pain of that moment, I recalled an assignment I had written during my first year at university, revealing the feminine characteristics I most admired. I felt moved to revisit those innocent sentiments on paper, but I had long ago mislaid that early, awkward attempt at the art of writing.

"Not that it matters one whit, Holmes," I suggested on returning to my arm-chair and adopting a hopelessly inept air of nonchalance, "what was your objection to the young lady's inquiry?"

"The banality of it all, Watson!" Holmes blared. "All cats up trees and lost waifs! This is the situation to which Sherlock Holmes is reduced."

"But the murder of the man servant has, as you would put it, an air of the 'outré.'"

"Listen, my boy, we recently shared a great adventure, did we not?"

"You know I intend to publish it."

"Then you, more than any other living soul, must appreciate that my powers have been tested to the extreme and that I exceeded my wildest expectations of myself. Now, I yearn for greater challenges. I ask you, Watson, am I to succumb to cases of petty theft and lost waifs?"

"I understand," I said, slightly alarmed at how full Holmes was of himself at present. However, he *was* young. Thinking of him as such was difficult at times, his manner generally so severe and stilted that one's initial impression of him was of an individual of far greater age. In a metaphysical frame of mind one might even have said that he was "an old soul" in the body of a young man. It was the rare occurrence when an impulsive or inappropriate action betrayed that youthfulness.

Attempting to lighten the mood, I remarked, "Miss Gates certainly possessed a beauty of some rare dimension."

"I had not noticed," Holmes curtly replied.

I could not but contrast his indifference to the charms of the young woman who had graced our rooms with my frenzied desire to be once more in her presence.

"I know, Holmes," said I, picturing her features before me. "To you, the precision of a Euclidean problem is of far greater beauty than that of any oval face of creamiest complexion."

With index finger stabbing at the air, Holmes replied, "I *am* encouraged. You are beginning to understand the proper relationship of women to the world."

Holmes had moved to the sofa and was now shifting shag tobacco from the toe-end of the oriental slipper to the blackened bowl of his pipe whilst whistling a favorite piece by Mendelsohn. I saw no point in continuing to champion the young woman's cause. Instead, my thoughts turned to the sorry woman I had met halfway up the stairs.

"As to that missing little girl," I proffered, clearing my throat.

"Please, Watson," Holmes snapped back.

"Could we not set the irregulars on this matter, Holmes?"

"If I accepted that woman's case, I would soon be following errant spouses down grimy alleyways, Watson. One thing leads to another in this world. I cannot risk my reputation for one grubby little girl. She shall show up, Watson, I assure you."

Lost in feelings of hopelessness, I turned my thoughts to Lucy Gates: Her slender, nervous fingers, the natural, aristocratic tilt of the head. How I longed to spend a moment more with her!

"Holmes," I abruptly announced, "I must take my leave. An urgent matter!"

"But Watson!" Holmes exclaimed, "I was about to query you upon a point."

"Surely," I rebuffed moving to the door, "the matter can wait till my return."

"As you wish," Holmes grimly replied with a shrug.

No sooner had he uttered these words than an image arose in my mind's eye: The nickel-plated syringe gleaming in mid-air, a seven percent solution lapping at the piston and a drop, like dew, welling at the slanted tip of the vicious needle. I spun round, momentarily reigning in thoughts of Lucy Gates, and approached Holmes, saying, "Forgive my thoughtlessness. Had you something on your mind?"

Holmes moved to the closet, pulled on his tweed overcoat and donned a favorite cap.

"For now," Holmes declared, "I starve. I'm off to the Cat and Pudding for an overdue breakfast. Join me if you like."

CHAPTER 2

A Mystery Unfolds

I had accompanied Mr. Sherlock Holmes to one of his favourite taverns, deciding in the interests of domestic tranquility to let matters lie and to postpone an attempt to locate my Juliet. Returning to our rooms, Holmes settled into an amiable disposition with a pipeful of *Ship's* and a review of the morning news.

Suddenly clapping his hands, he exclaimed, "Was I not about to discuss a matter with you, Watson, when—"

Just then, Mrs. Hudson gave her distinctive knock on the door.

"Sorry, gentlemen," said she, "I thought that was the lot for the morning, but a gentleman just appeared at the door. I thought of shooing him away, really I did. But he's most distressed, Mr. Holmes. I hadn't the heart. I decided I'd best leave the matter up to you."

"Mrs. Hudson, what shall we do with you? The bracing challenge of a missing dog or stray spouse, no doubt," Holmes sneered under his breath. "Very well," he yielded, "send him in."

A white-haired, weathered man entered our sitting-room with what I could only imagine to be the rambling saunter of a cowhand, a twitch in his left eye, a frayed cap in hand.

Holmes declared, "I am Sherlock Holmes. May I be of assistance?"

Clearing his throat, the elderly gentleman looked up at Holmes with a squint and croaked, "Well, sir, some jokers broke down my door last night."

"Ah, the theft of a valuable?" Holmes cheekily inquired with a wink in my direction.

"Yer darn tootin'."

"Darn tootin'," Holmes mocked under his breath. "And this something of value?"

"Most beauty full thing ever I set eyes on, gents. One of them new type-writin' machines."

I had never observed Holmes so taken aback. He rose from the sofa and pressed the back as if to steady himself.

"A typewriter, you say?" With arched brow, Holmes looked my way and licked his lips with anticipatory delight.

"Yes, sir. One day I was alookin' through the paper and spotted an ad about the contraption. All them levers and buttons! Ever since, I had my eye on one to give my granddaughter. For her schoolin,' y'understand. Didn't want her to go through what I had to. Scraped up the money, bought the danged thing, and now it's gone!"

"I see," said Holmes. "And nothing else stolen?"

"Nothin' left worth stealin,' Mr. Holmes! Don't take a brain to see I'm a dirt poor man. Now, at least. Oh, years back I worked a couple of claims back in the states, Mohave desert thereabouts. Spent the gold dust on women and gamblin' houses till it dried up. Worked all my danged life to wind up dragged here by a fool friend with schemes that went south. Nothin' left now for me or my granddaughter."

"I am sorry," commiserated Holmes. "The chance of finding one typewriting machine in the whole of London is slim, my good man," explained Holmes. "You see that, I'm sure. You would do better reporting the theft to the proper authorities."

"S'pose you're right," the elderly gentleman aquiesced, "Guess I'll never see that thing again. Thanks jus' the same." Plopping the battered cap on his white-mopped head, he shuffled out and down the stairs.

Holmes leapt to my side, fire in his eyes, exclaiming, "What do you say to that, Watson? Something singular is occurring in this drab city of ours! What be the chance, dear friend, of two such inquiries on the self-same morning by pure coincidence?"

"Exceedingly slim," I replied, finding Holmes' excitement contagious.

"Slim? Nearer to nil, my friend! This matter of stolen typewriters intrigues me, Watson. Give me your thoughts on the problem."

"It is puzzling."

"Puzzling, yes. To break into a home when other valuables—smaller, more easily disposable—are at hand." The flame of Holmes' match splashed the sharp features of his face with a momentary golden flicker as he added, "I must admit, this little puzzler, these purloined typewriters, has me in its grip. Be that as it may.

"Watson," he suddenly exclaimed with raised index finger and rare youthful exuberance, "come with me on holiday!"

"Holiday?" I repeated, dumbfounded. "Of all the time…"

"You surprise me, Watson. Don't you think I have earned some slight reward?"

"Of course, Holmes, but—"

"Did I so poorly in your eyes? Can you not recall, as I can, each singular event of our recent adventure? That fateful summons on a gray morning by Gregson of Scotland Yard: E. J. Drebber's grotesque, cold body at Three Lauriston Gardens: The word 'rache' inscribed in blood on the peeling wall: Joseph Stangerson's murder the following morning: And then my shamelessly melodramatic capture of the murderer, one Jefferson Hope, before the startled eyes of Messieurs Lestrade and Gregson in these very rooms: And all the blessed moments in between.

"Surely, you of all people," and here Holmes twisted round in his arm-chair in the direction of the vile drawer wherein he stored the needle and cocaine, "—given the alternative—should find an excursion the healthier choice. And who save you, trusted companion, should accompany me?"

A momentary lull in conversation passed when Holmes dryly declared, "After all, Watson. Are you and your colleagues not apt to suggest a trip to your patients on the slightest provocation?"

"Not without good cause," I countered.

"Could it be?" Holmes now muttered to himself as though struck by a revelation. "No, the idea is too fantastic!"

"What idea?" I was foolish enough to ask.

"Could a dark conspiracy possibly exist between the medical and travel professions to enhance a handsome source of revenue?"

Thoughts of losing Lucy Gates to a petty trek across the continent had already incited my displeasure; the charge Holmes now so recklessly made proved the proverbial "last straw." Indeed, I had actually sprung to my feet to protest his careless allegation—my face florid with indignation, the old Jezail bullet wound to my shoulder throbbing anew—when I noticed the wry smile spreading across his face. I realized in time that his remark had been made in jest.

In the brief span of our friendship, Holmes' remarkable histrionic abilities had more than once caught me off my guard. We laughed heartily and agreed that the hour had come for brisk preparation of our upcoming trip, even as I vowed to myself that my pursuit of Lucy Gates would be delayed but a day.

CHAPTER 3

The Lady Vanishes

An acquaintance in whom I had confided my plans suggested delaying the journey until the route of the *Chemin de Fer Orientaux* was completed to Istanbul. But given the unstable political situation in the East, no one could guarantee how long such an undertaking should take to complete; I decided to follow the itinerary as originally proposed by Holmes.

Even as I busied myself securing accommodations, the face of Lucy Gates rose again and again before my eyes. I decided to visit a colleague, a Dr. Bell, to peruse his not insubstantial collection of directories and registries in the hope of finding the young lady's name therein, but to no avail.

Heading back to Baker Street, I remembered an acquaintance at the Official Registry. I made my way to a district messenger office and sent a wire imploring him for the name and address of the cabman who had so brusquely whisked away the young woman from my sight.

When I returned home mid-afternoon, Holmes was in the midst of one of his noxious experiments. In the best of moods, I found these episodes irksome, but under the stress of awaiting some reply to my wire my tolerance had grown quite brittle. With a slam of the door, I locked myself in my room where I continued my vigil alone into the evening.

Mrs. Hudson finally brought up dinner. Only telegrams confirming our itinerary arrived; I dined in silence whilst Holmes scratched upon a note-pad between bites.

"Is anything the matter?" he asked. "You seem ill-at-ease."

"Nothing of the kind," I curtly replied.

What words might I call forth, I wondered, to help Holmes understand how important finding Lucy Gates had become for me in so short a time? His was a bloodless world of analysis, pure cause and effect, and little else save his passion for scratching upon his prized Stradivarius. As far as I knew, Mrs. Hudson was the one female in his life, and I had never heard Holmes mention a past relationship with a member of the opposite sex. Even in our most intimate moments, I had yet to muster the nerve to delve into that privacy which Holmes so earnestly protected.

Just as I was finishing dinner, the landlady brought up the wire which I had been anxiously awaiting. I tore it open to read the following words:

> In answer to your query, the Excelsior Cab Company records that cab number 195 delivered a young lady to 32 Campton Lane at approximately ten o'clock this morning.

I suddenly boomed, "I must away, Holmes," and hurriedly abandoned my puzzled friend to finish his dinner alone. I could not find a cab quickly enough nor walk the few paces and the few stairsteps up to her door fast enough to suit my pounding heart. And despite my joy at finding myself before her very rooms, a sudden, crushing sense of doom caused me to approach the door with trepidation. I timidly rapped the knocker.

A tense moment passed till a crack in the door appeared, and I beheld the vivid blue eyes of Lucy Gates peering past the chasm into my admiring glance. A spark of recognition was evident upon her expression, and Lucy Gates widened the gap so that I might view her delicate frame.

"Dr. Watson," she declared, "what a surprise."

"Is it?" I replied.

"Why, yes," said she apprehensively, her gaze looking past me, as though to survey what lay in the distance.

"May I?" I said, taking a step forward when she swung the door to a crack to block my entry.

"I am sorry, Dr. Watson," she said with furrowed brow, "but I am expecting a visitor at any moment." Her gaze fell to the floor with these words.

"I am concerned for your welfare, Miss Gates. I feel you are in some danger. I wish to…help."

She looked up at me with disarming frankness as she asked, "But why, Dr. Watson, should my well-being be of any interest to you?"

"I...I believe that I am falling in love with you, Lucy Gates," I boldly declared.

"Then, John," her hand reaching out to grasp mine as she continued, "I may call you John?"

"Yes, of course, Lucy," I replied.

"Then, John, return to-night at eleven and we may talk then."

"If you are in some danger," I declared, "I am bound to stay, Lucy!"

"I shall be all right, John," she assured me. "Return at eleven and I shall explain my actions and the device."

"Device?"

"The typewriter, I mean. I shall explain later. Go now, please. Return to-night, my good Doctor."

I turned round and began descending the short flight of steps when her voice called to me.

"John," said she, "I am truly glad you found me," and clicked the door shut. With her proclamation of affection echoing in my ears, my heart skipped a beat. I felt the schoolboy, again, with that unnerving mix of agony and ecstasy. Nothing in this world would stop me from returning at eleven as she had requested.

I decided to pass the time at my club. I sank into the plush red leather of a corner arm-chair, my mind awhirl.

I was inclined to believe that Lucy was in harm's way, and I considered whether or not to involve Holmes. With the promise of some privacy when next I met Lucy, could I rob the two of us of this prospect by Holmes' presence? Nay, with Lucy's safety uppermost in my mind, could I risk not involving Holmes?

The moment had come to hail a cab. A light rain began to fall as the driver pulled up to Campton Lane. I reached the door and knocked to no answer. I realized that no light shown through the windowpanes, and panic shot through me as I rapped now with full force and called out Lucy's name. No answer returned.

In a frenzy, I decided to seek what light Holmes should shed on my mystery, but by the time I reached our sitting-room he had assembled that rag-tag lot of street arabs he affectionately dubbed the irregulars. From past experience, my first move was to discretely part the windows to their widest perimeter; personal hygiene was not amongst the irregulars' virtues.

With a broad smile, Holmes set his eyes upon the tall, flaxen-haired youth to his right. "Tommy, as usual, I shall entrust you to station the right men for the job."

"Yes, sir," Tommy crisply replied, snapping to attention whilst returning Holmes' warm smile.

"Now men," Holmes continued, "let us review some possible strategies…"

I could see that Holmes was not about to end the conference anytime soon, and I had no intention of interrupting his efforts. I surreptitiously made my way to the door for a quick exit when I felt Holmes' strong hand on my shoulder.

"Don't leave, Watson," he implored. "I see that you are troubled and that you seek a friend's guidance."

Turning round, I replied, "True, Holmes. But how in God's name—"

"The language of the body," explained Holmes, "never lies. It is an art mastered by every accomplished stage actor. And I intend—" Holmes turned round to the raucous sound of horseplay, "hold on, men—I intend to make it a science and the subject of a future monograph."

He led me to our arm-chair and signaled me to wait as he rejoined the motley band now scattered throughout the room.

"And so, men," Holmes declared in that mock military manner he often adopted when addressing his special aides, as much to add a humorous touch as to secure their wandering attention, "I have shared this mystery of the typewriting machines with you, every fact—in fact—," and here giggles rippled through the band of raucous boys, "to which I am also privileged. Be bold, men," added Holmes to the assemblage, "but above all stay safe. Remember your mission: To discover as many incidents of stolen machines as you can. Tommy, distribute these coins amongst the men. Evenly! There, then, it's off with you all!"

With a doffed cap or two and salutations the like of "See you, Mr. 'olmes" and "Goo' night, Dr. Watson," the rag-tag band made a tumultuous egress down the stairs and out the front door, leaving Holmes and me alone at last.

"So, Watson," Holmes exclaimed, sinking into our sofa as he ignited a cigarette, "is this a one pipe problem, or should I order from the tobacconist?"

"I think not, Holmes," I replied with a tepid smile.

Holmes looked at me with that commanding expression that demanded reply.

"Lucy Gates has disappeared, Holmes."

"Ah, the young lady whose typewriter was stolen."

"Therein lies another mystery. She made reference to a device."

"I thought I detected evasion during her interview. Hmmm…device…characters…numerals…calculations. Watson, I have a feeling that the item was not a conventional typewriter. I remember filing away an article concerning—" Holmes suddenly leapt to his voluminous collection of notes and odd facts gathered from every source imaginable, his slender, nervous fingers racing through a blur of pages.

"Aha," he declared, a sheet of paper bobbing nervously in his sinewy hand, "listen to this, Watson. One Charles Babbage…member of the Royal Astronomical Society…an extraordinary polymath…inventor, mathematician, philosopher…designed footwear for walking on water, fascinating…suggested speaking tubes to link London and Liverpool together. And look here, Watson. Constructed several machines he referred to as 'difference engines' to automate complex calculations. Here, I think, is your device! And a partial solution to why one kills for a typewriter."

"I beg your pardon."

"When is a typewriter not a typewriter, Watson? When it is a calculating device of inestimable powers. Somone's agents, for lack of brains, is mistaking this device for a typewriting machine."

Holmes cleared his throat and moved to my side. "And so, what have Lucy Gates and the theft of a calculating device to do with John Watson, late of the 5th Regiment of Foot in Afghanistan?"

"I…I am smitten," I sheepishly admitted. "Can you understand that, Holmes?"

"Ah, a complication. Romance rears its ugly head."

Holmes' flippant manner inflamed my ire, and I lashed back.

"The matter is serious, Holmes. She is missing. We must postpone our plans. We must find her."

"Now that I have set my mind upon the journey?" retorted Holmes. "Little chance, Watson. You and I shall holiday as planned whilst my little helpers take on one more challenge."

"But, Holmes," I admitted with broken voice, "I fear for her life."

"You say that she is missing, Watson. When you visited her, did you detect any signs of violence?"

"I can not say that I did."

"Then she is not missing so much as simply not where you expected her to be."

Holmes stood and pulled the window-shade aside to peer into the black void that was Baker Street in the dead of night.

"A classic example," Holmes gibed, "of the tenderer emotions clouding one's mind, Watson. Allay your fears, dear friend," he said confidently, patting a yawn with the back of the hand.

"But Holmes," I entreated, "Lucy Gates!"

"Really, Watson," Holmes decried, "the way you go on. You hardly know the woman. You know only a mask."

"This is, perhaps, a subject outside your experience."

"Perhaps," replied Holmes stoically. To my surprise, I thought that I saw his eyes mist over as he repeated, "Perhaps." He turned his back to me as he continued, "If Lucy Gates may be found, our irregulars shall surely find her. Now the hour is late, Watson. It's to bed."

Further efforts of my own to find Lucy were beyond my powers. Holmes seemed supremely confident that she was in no real danger and that the irregulars would discover her whereabouts. He was determined to undertake the journey already planned. And so, dejected and filled with self-loathing, I let the matter pass despite the shadow that had now fallen on the young woman's safety and my happiness. Weary to the bone, I fell deeply asleep.

Lucy Gates and I danced an endless waltz in a great empty, mirrored hall under an impossibly high gilt ceiling.

CHAPTER 4

The Metaphysician

Thursday morning found Holmes and me standing by the gleaming rails of Victoria Station, engulfed in a pageant of colour and motion: Persons of all stations in life about their various ways with equal earnestness, the plans of the baker and of the candlestick-maker no less than the most intricate machinations of highest office or of noblest rank.

The hour had come to board the train. One last time, I swept my eyes across the span of the bustling station in childlike expectation that the face of my Lucy Gates should suddenly meet my gaze. Holmes and I settled into our first-class carriage, and soon we were pulling out of Victoria. The train gently rocked us to and fro, the morning edition of the paper rustling in our hands as we leisurely perused the world news.

From the corner of my eye, I caught Holmes stealthily turning to the agony column—that dreadful collection of personal advertisements to which he so often referred during a case—and loudly cleared my throat in protestation. Holmes acknowledged my admonition with good humour, set that section of the paper aside and continued with the balance, though I could not help but note with amusement his eye occasionally transgressing in the direction of the forbidden text jostling by his side.

After many a delightful discussion with my friend, several cups of tea, coffee and bits of food, the time had come to embark on the ferry at Folkestone for the trip across the channel. Holmes and I stood on the open deck noting the timeless majesty of the cliffs of Dover and the approaching coast of France.

The ship berthed in Boulogne whence we secured our new cabin for the train to Paris, alighting in the dazzling city well in time for dinner.

We settled into our over-night accommodations, then walked briskly in the direction of *L'Étoile*, a restaurant just off the Seine and highly recommended by a colleague for its superior fare. Holmes and I were seated promptly whereupon I was taken aback by Holmes' delicacy of palate when the time came to choose from a French menu. He would not touch the *escargots,* righteously decreeing that snails were meant for testing one's sure-footedness on rain-soaked pavement but not for ingesting at any meal. On our way back to the hotel, we made it a point to enjoy the sight of the Seine's waters rushing along its banks, as it had for countless generations. Back in our rooms, I thought it appropriate to attempt to teach Holmes the delights of playing *écarté* but after a half-hour of frustration I relented, allowing my friend his enjoyment of a cigarette before we retired.

In the morning, I had to knock up Holmes with several violent shakes of the bed. He disappeared to check for any wires from the irregulars, but the look of disappointment upon his face on his return spoke volumes. After a breakfast of croissants and strong black coffee served in our room, we boarded our carriage at *La Gare de Strasbourg* and were on the move, again.

Luckily the accommodations of our carriage were comfortable, and we found the menu and service in the dining-car more than satisfactory. Halfway through my meal, however, I called upon the *chef de brigade* to complain of finding a hair, rather coarse and grey-brown, under the sauce of my entrée. The plate was dispatched forthwith with a fresh, steaming platter served in its stead. Unfortunately, by then, Holmes' appetite seemed to have suffered.

"I don't mean to spoil the remainder of your meal, Watson," Holmes whispered, "but my strong conviction is that the hair you found had at one time been attached to a rat."

"Rat?" I repeated, nonchalantly.

"Yes," Holmes replied, puzzlement in his voice to my indifference. "I have written a modest monograph on varieties of hair, should you recall, Watson."

"I see," I said between bites. "Put your mind at ease, dear Holmes. Ate many a rat during the war. Tastes rather like…game hen." With this remark, Holmes pushed away his plate whilst I continued enjoying the contents of mine to completion.

Soon, Holmes and I were jostling back toward our cabin to relax with a good smoke. Before boarding, I had purchased a box of particularly fine Havana cigars, the kind I enjoy on a special occasion, and began preparing one. I had expected Holmes to produce one of his beloved pipes. Instead, he withdrew a snuffbox from his waist-coat, a great amethyst on the deeply engraved, golden lid, and lifted a pinch of the nut-brown flakes to his nose. I recalled that the snuffbox had been a prize for Holmes' discreet services to one of the royal families of Europe.

I looked forward to our arrival in Vienna, one of the focal points of our trip, and from there to exploring the spas that we had discussed in making our plans. Karlovy Vary west of Prague was of particular interest to me as a medical man. I was especially curious as to whether the sulfurous waters were as distasteful and medicinal as I had been led to believe by colleagues.

Mile upon mile of scenery passed before us. I noted that upon leaving Munich the country had taken on a distinctively Austrian character, and, like a spell-bound child, I excitedly pointed out to Holmes every fairy-tale cottage that came into view.

At last we arrived in Vienna late in the evening. Holmes and I found our way to the comfortable hotel I had engaged by wire. Its only real disadvantage was in being some too few blocks from a wondrous shop stocked with pastries bursting with butter, sugar and wild berries ablaze with colour. Holmes was never one for dessert, but I convinced him to accompany me for a late-night treat.

Holmes could not be persuaded to order anything but a demi-tasse whilst I indulged my sweet tooth in a miniature masterpiece of almond paste drizzled in dark chocolate. Satisfied, we moved briskly to exit when a little man had the misfortune to suddenly place his person in the very spot in which Holmes and I had just stepped. With a sharp thud, he spilled to the pavement just outside the entrance to the shop. Holmes and I fell to his rescue with effusive apologies.

"Are you all right?" I asked, offering my arm.

"I…think," he replied in a dazed tone of voice and with a heavy guttural accent.

"I am a doctor, sir. Perhaps I should make a cursory inspection of your person, with your permission. Holmes, have you any objection to my turning our sitting-room into a temporary consulting-room?"

"Not a bit, Watson," replied Holmes. "After all, how many times have I made that very request of you?"

The little man seemed to enjoy our attentions and allowed us to fetch a cab for the few blocks to our rooms. Along the way, he informed us that his name was Ernst Klauske and declared that he was a "metaphysician." But when he began prattling about the psychic meaning of colours in the rainbow, I feared that he had suffered a concussion in the fall.

It was not until we entered our room, however, and had lit a couple of lamps that I came to appreciate the abject shabbiness of the little man's appearance, his clothes much the worse for wear and crudely patched in several places. He reeked as well of a strong, disagreeable anise-like stench. Despite his pitiable state, my overriding thought was of his well-being.

As I began my examination, the little man entertained us with a rather earthy perspective of Viennese history and a rambling discourse on the mystical significance of raindrops. The sickly anise-tainted odour coming from his breath had me nearly swooning, but I continued my inspection until I was satisfied that his physical state had not been compromised.

"But for a bruise or two, Herr Klauske, I may safely say you are in excellent condition."

A burden seemed to lift from the little man's animated face, and in gratitude he implored us to join him in a drink at a nearby favourite tavern. Seeing that he was unwilling to take no for an answer, Holmes and I acquiesced with a shrug of our shoulders, accepting his homely invitation with as much grace as the hour permitted.

With Klauske assuring us that he was up to the walk, we three scrambled along the worn, cobbled streets of Vienna, winding through a maze of evil-smelling alley-ways til we stood before the greasy, well-worn door of a tavern named the Tav. A skeleton of a man swung the door ajar, gave a rattling breath or two as he spilled out onto the street and shook his head as though to clear a fog from his mind. His eyes were glazed over and sunk deep within his face as I saw him sway to and fro, then disappear with a halting gait into the blackness of a sinister lane.

Holmes suddenly snapped his head to the side as if spotting movement out of the corner of his eye. Glancing in that direction, I, too, caught the trace of a shadow before it slid hastily out of view. By then, Klauske was motioning us to make after him through the portal to a small, spotted table in a corner of the smoke-laden room. The dank and squalour recalled an unfortunate errand I once undertook in search of a friend that led me to a notorious opium den in a singular unsavoury section of Whitechapel.

Out of the gloom, a burly waiter stepped forward and with a dull thud slapped a cloudy flask of emerald green liqueur on the table. He tossed three slotted spoons, a bowl of shaved ice and three soiled shot glasses beside the flask with a clatter.

"I am being grateful for your company, gentlemen," Klauske said. "You see, I am something of a connoisseur of absinthe, and this, my friends, is the finest of the fine; it is all they serve here. Only the creme of Viennese society come here to savour this ambrosia!"

Holmes could scarcely contain a laugh, looking about at the assemblage of dour patrons through a brown haze of smoke, their dull eyes seemingly pinned on the drinks in hand.

"You know, Watson," Holmes whispered in my ear, "I am not as perverse as you may have been led to believe. I have never tasted absinthe," he admitted, sniffing curiously at the lip of the flask.

The little man carefully poured a bright stream into each of our glasses as though portioning out gold dust. The strong, now familiar smell of anise rose strongly from the emerald pools in the glasses. We watched as Klauske undertook a small ritual with some solemnity, placing ice in one of the slotted spoons which he held above the absinthe. Drops of icy water dripped slowly into the verdant pool below, which Klauske then sipped with obvious delight.

With sadness, he noted that we had not chosen the most fortuitous time to visit Vienna. We had missed, for instance, the impressive foot-washing ceremony held at Easter when members of the Royal family invite twelve men and twelve women of low status to the Palace of the Hofburg. They are offered, so the little man explained, sumptuous banquets. Then, as the *Oberst-Ceremonien-Meister* announces the Emperor and the Imperial family, the shoes and stockings of these lowly guests are removed for a ceremonial washing by the Imperial household whilst the Court Chaplain recites The Last Supper from the Gospel. Before the festivities end, each of the twenty-four guests is given a hefty bag of silver coins and groaning baskets of food saved from the banquet tables. As the little man concluded his intriguing sketch, he withdrew from his pocket a silver coin to display before us, a prideful grin upon his face. Green glints of reflected light shot off the edges of the medallion.

We had also arrived too early, according to our remarkable guest, to witness the splendour of the Danube frozen over, ladies in rich furs and velvet, bejeweled and draped in delicate lace, riding in fanciful sleighs of fantastic animal forms—griffins, camels, tigers—each sleigh driven by a single, steaming, bejeweled horse.

Holmes—at times of a most egalitarian turn—seemed to warm to our peculiar guest and invited him to return to his metaphysical theories whilst I circumspectly sampled the strange, green liqueur. The little man relayed some notions of his—preposterous in the extreme—concerning the meaning of colours in human "auras," which he claimed to see radiating from Holmes and me at that very moment.

"Do you mean to say," inquired Holmes, with genuine interest, "that you perceive some sort of 'emanation' illuminating our bodies, sir?"

"Oh, yes, Herr Holmes," the little man replied with growing animation. "I see a pageant of reds and yellows blasting from your person."

"And what of mine?" I inquired.

"Brown, sir, very brown."

I began doubting my earlier diagnosis of his condition lest his outlandish theorizing was the result of the potent beverage he had been sipping with such gusto.

"Let me see your hands," Klauske suddenly demanded of Holmes with a forcefulness in his voice I had not previously detected. A shudder seemed to attack his whole frame at the moment Holmes offered his hands palm-up.

"Herr Holmes," Klauske said slowly and intensely, "be of great care. I see danger, terrible danger."

Holmes' expression seemed one of mild interest rather than of alarm as he requested in a staccato voice, "Pray continue."

"Are you in the dangerous professions, Herr Holmes?"

"Surely you have read my name in the papers."

"No, I do not mean to make the offense, Herr Holmes. I do not know your past. But I know a little of your future. And great danger is coming to you. Perhaps to your friend," Klauske added, turning dramatically in my direction. "I beg of you both, take me seriously, gentlemen."

"Do you see anything else, Herr Klauske?" asked Holmes with a slight yawn, seemingly impatient now of the little man's company.

"Beware unseen waters, gentlemen."

"We are planning to sample the waters of certain spas in the area," Holmes said disdainfully, "but I suspect you do not refer to them."

"Unseen." Klauske's eyes turned to slits. "Beware, my friends. A flood of waters that you cannot see. A mountain so high it is capped by clouds. Explosions, terrible explosions! Death and destruction!"

By now I had had enough of both the little man and the vile drink of which I had taken but a couple of cursory sips. Holmes, too, appeared eager to depart and to return to the healthy confines of our hotel. As Holmes and I prepared to exit, to Herr Klauske I suggested bed-rest for at least a couple of days and made our apologies for having to take our leave.

As we turned to the door, he grasped the hem of Holmes' sleeve, looked intensely into the slate-grey eyes and exclaimed, "You are an 'old soul,' you are living many lives past, Herr Holmes, and if you heed the advice, you will be living a long and prosperous life in this world." With a nod, Holmes delicately removed the man's hand and led our way out the tavern.

Back in our rooms, Holmes exclaimed, "Well, Watson, what do you make of that?"

"A concussion, a slight bruise to the brain, that is all, Holmes. Don't let the ravings of that pathetic man trouble you or ruin your enjoyment of a long-deserved holiday. But Holmes, did you not eye something unusual back at that tavern, just before we entered?"

"And I thought we weren't to discuss anything so plebeian as work?"

"In all seriousness, I myself thought that someone's shadow had raced away into the dark."

"The night is full of shadows," Holmes declared. "Do not allow a shadow to fall upon our trip. Put your mind at ease, dear Watson."

We talked on, sipping *slivovice* until it was past mid-night. With morning I again visited the nearby shop, returning to our rooms with a boxful of delights for breakfast, but Holmes would have nothing but tea. We spent the remainder of the day sight-seeing, finding ourselves by dusk along *Haupt Alléc* with her rows of stately chestnut trees and her *cafés* teeming with the fashionable and wealthy of Viennese society. Exhausted, we chose to rest for the journey northward toward Prague which we would face to-morrow.

"I must say, Watson," confessed Holmes, back in the comfort of our room, "spending time together was a splendid idea of mine. Years from now, who knows where we shall be? You, for example, might be a proud grandfather—children dangling off your knees—too occupied to offer a trusted, old friend some of the companionship he once took so for granted. And who's to know—save our unsavory friend somewhere in Vienna—where I shall be?" he added, wistfully.

Holmes' last remark brought my thoughts round to the little man's warnings.

"Holmes," I was compelled to ask before retiring, "you don't suppose that that strange little man could truly foresee the future, pull aside the veil of to-morrow in some manner unknown to us and look upon impending tragedy?"

"My dear Watson, he knew who I am and very probably who you are. Despite his appearance, he seemed a man of some education, could certainly read the papers and performed some subtle legerdemain, not too dissimilar to what I do with facts and deductive reasoning during a case. Was it so great a leap, then, to see danger for a man with a reputation for championing against the criminal class? No, put your mind to rest. Ours shall be an uneventful trip, precisely what we both sorely need."

"You put me at ease, Holmes."

We quietly enjoyed a cigarette together. In my room, I changed and returned to the sitting-room to wish Holmes a good-night. As I moved back to the door of my room, Holmes dryly said, "I have been sitting here considering whether to share something with you, Watson, and I think I shall. I have been conducting experiments of my own to pull aside 'the veil,' as you so colourfully put it. Would you be willing to put my newfound powers to the test? Excellent, kindly locate those pasteboards you were so insistent I play in our Paris accommodations."

"They are here, Holmes!" I said excitedly.

"The night is drawing near. Let me pull a few cards aside, these five then, to save time." Holmes laid them face up on the tea-tray before me. "Now, my boy, look these cards over, and in your mind alone choose one and one only. Take care that you don't inadvertently mouth the chosen card to yourself or turn your eye in its direction."

"It is done, Holmes," I said, playing along.

"Now, I have more than once put before you some sly tricks employed by the charlatan and by the professional necromancer, at such time I deemed it appropriate to apply some subterfuge to force a successful resolution to an adventure of ours.

"For example, practitioners of parlour-tricks have long known that certain cards come more readily to mind than others. The Queen of Hearts is a favourite with the ladies, I am told. Should you ask a group of the fairer sex to think of a card, astoundingly, most select the Queen of Hearts, and a man of devious persuasion or a clever entertainer might take advantage of this secret knowledge to create an extraordinary effect. So that such a possibility is dismissed in the case of our little experiment, I should like you to now clear your mind and make yet a second choice from amongst the five cards, keeping in mind my previous admonitions."

"Very well," I said.

"Take me into your confidence now, dear Watson, and reveal the card you chose the second time round."

"Why, it was the Deuce of Hearts, Holmes. Where," I asked laughing, "is the mystery in that?"

Holmes sucked in a deep breath of satisfaction and sank into his chair whilst nodding his head. "My dear Watson, before you ever laid eyes on this row of five cards, I secured a prediction beneath the tea-tray where I could not alter the message after the fact. Be so kind as to lift the tray."

Underneath, I discovered a small scrap of foolscap, neatly folded in quarters. Unfolding it, my eyes widened as I read the note, which in my utter astonishment I let slip from my fingers.

"Well, Watson," Holmes requested, "please do me the courtesy of reading my note aloud, if you please."

Retrieving the slip of paper, I muttered the following words written in Holmes' distinctive hand:

Dear Watson,

The second card you choose shall be the Deuce of Hearts.

Yours, S.H.

My mind swooned with the revelation of my companion's new powers. "Holmes, this goes beyond…I don't know what to think or to say! Save that this proves that we should put new credence in what the little Austrian warned."

Holmes doubled up in an uncharacteristic convulsion of raucous laughter.

"Forgive me, Watson, these poor theatrics," he confessed, slapping his knee. "I had to force the point to dismiss from your mind the little man's warnings."

"But Holmes, your prediction. You *have* pulled aside the veil."

"Be so kind as to lift the cushion beneath you," said Holmes.

Underneath was an identical piece of foolscap, but when I unfolded it, the note written in Holmes' hand named the Knave of Spades, another of the five, face-up cards on the tea-tray.

"And now, lift the lamp by the door, Watson."

Yet another of Holmes' predictions named the Four of Clubs.

"You see, Watson, what effect may be derived from so simple a device? Look beneath the table-cloth there, and you shall find my prediction for the fourth card and under the rug my prediction for the last of the pasteboards I pulled from the deck."

"I still don't think I understand," I admitted.

"Dear Watson, I fear the young lady is still clouding your mind. Women and deduction do not mix, I assure you. Had you disclosed the Six of Diamonds, rather than ask you to lift the tea-tray, I should have asked you to go to the throw-rug and discover the prediction I made for that card in your absence."

Shaking my head, I said, "It is so simple, Holmes, now that you have explained your method."

"As simple as my most startling revelations during the course of a case, eh, Watson?"

"Holmes, you have left the music halls poorer for your interest in crime over the theatre."

"Your mind is at rest, then?"

"It is," said I.

"You will put aside the ravings of the little Austrian?"

"Yes," I answered, beaming silently for Holmes' display of concern.

"And Miss Gates?"

"That I cannot promise."

"Very well. Good-night, then, Watson."

"Good-night, Holmes."

That night, Lucy Gates and I danced again to a Viennese waltz. But carnival was in the air, and one of the masqueraders was the little Austrian in the guise of the Joker cartwheeling around us. Looking down, I admired myself as the Ace of Spades, and in my arms danced Lucy, Queen of Hearts. Suddenly we were all gathered together by unseen hands and shuffled, cut and shuffled, cut and shuffled like so many pasteboards…

CHAPTER 5

The Mendicant Friar

Sherlock Holmes and I left Vienna on one of the narrow gauge railways criss-crossing the Austrian state and operated by the *Kaiserlich und Koeniglich Staats Bahnen*. My enjoyment of the passing scenery, however, was being interrupted by the incessant buzz of a fly. I had my eye on it, and Holmes had his eye on me. The fly settled to within striking distance on the seat beside me as I rolled *The Times* into an instrument of death. Taking aim, I raised my arm with pantherlike cunning when Holmes' voice disrupted my concentration, and the fly buzzed away.

"I don't know that you should indiscriminately kill a friend of ours," he wryly said, "such as that roguish fly."

"Friend, indeed," I retorted indignantly. "That friend so-called has been tormenting me for some twenty minutes."

"Ah, but I have been investigating the phenomenon of flies at the scene of a murder, Watson. If only you knew how invaluable they can be to one seeking the truth." Holmes puffed nonchalantly on his pipe, sending blue plumes of twisting smoke into the cabin air. "Please be candid. Had I mentioned any of this previously?"

"Why no, Holmes," I said, my interest peaking.

"I thought not." He continued, abstractly pulling on his pipe.

"Well?"

"I believe it shall lead to some assistance in the future. But no matter."

"Come now, Holmes." He had drawn me in mercilessly. "I beg of you, go on."

"You see, my dear Watson," Holmes continued with a sardonic laugh, "flies are often the first observers at the scene of a crime. I have determined that they are capable of detecting the odour of a corpse up to a mile away. Moreover, the female of the species may arrive and lay her eggs in the body. With the assistance of my street arabs I have conducted experiments using hares whose time and place of death had been kept from me. By applying my methods, examining the flies and maggots going about their enterprise on my unfortunate little victims, I have successfully determined a number of critical variables."

"Astounding!" I exclaimed.

"Indeed," Holmes added, and then a sly smile spread across his face. "Watson, there are even country flies and city flies."

"Now you jest, Holmes."

"No, I have conclusively proven the matter. Rest assured, should I ever find a rural maggot upon a city corpse I shall be confident in my opinion that the body had been moved."

It was then that I realized Holmes' devilish maneuver. "You have shrewdly allowed our conversation to drift into professional areas, and I shan't allow the situation to continue."

"Forgive me, Watson," said Holmes apologetically. "Better to enjoy the exquisite scenery passing before our window."

My companion and I took turns remarking upon the procession of Alpine vistas, highland splendours and quaint, story-book villages peopled by peasants in extraordinary costumes ablaze with colour and fantastic designs.

Holmes and I found the evening drawing near, and we moved to the dining-car. Though the room, in appointments, was not as luxurious as that of the *Compagne Internationale des Wagon-Lits*, we were satisfied nevertheless with our table and began earnestly studying the engraved menus handed us.

Our concentrated study of the entrées was diverted when we found the *chef de brigade* at over six foot tall standing by our table, a man of the cloth hiding self-consciously behind him.

"Excuse me, gentlemen, but the room is quite full, and I am asking for the Father if you would permit him to share your table."

"Delighted," said I, with a glance toward Holmes for a barely perceptible nod of his head. As I rose the Father begged me to be seated.

Holmes cleared his throat and declared, "I am Sherlock Holmes…"

My friend had a shockingly juvenile habit of adding the slightest of pauses to introductions of himself in the hope, I mused, of catching some sign of recognition in the addressed. "…and this," he continued, "my friend, Dr. John Watson."

"Th-thank you very m-much, gentlemen," said the Father, with no discernible acknowledgment in his voice of Holmes' reputation. "I am Father Mendel."

Sharing adventures with Holmes had not been in vain, allowing me to note telling detail at a glance with nearly the speed of the master. Seated across from me, for example, was a man of short, stocky build wearing round glasses on a round face. The high brow and thin lips suggested superior intellect, and I noted that he wore the distinctive vestments of the Augustinian monk.

"Holmes and I are traveling cross-country from London, Father. We are looking forward to seeing much of your splendid homeland."

"And there is so much to see, gentlemen. M-my trip, I'm afraid, has been one of business, though. The work of an abbot never stops.

"Gentlemen, the area is rich in history. Not far from my abbey lies the Napoleonic battlefield of Austerlitz. The entire region has long been a m-meeting place of East and West, and sometimes I imagine an entire procession on the move: Armies of Crusaders rumbling by, Mongol hordes looting and pillaging, cruel invaders from the dreaded Ottoman Empire slashing their way from victory to victory."

The Father's eyes had glossed over, moving to hidden vistas within his mind. Realizing that he had drifted into the realm of inmost visions, he returned to us, saying, "You must excuse me, gentlemen. I have a v-vivid immagination at times," Mendel confessed.

"A healthy attribute, Father," I replied.

"Perhaps. Please do not let me distract you from inspecting the menu…" Mendel hesitated on the last word until he managed the courage to express a hidden thought. "…lest you should care to have me order for you, some of the l-local foods and drink?"

With another of Holmes' stately nods, we left our gustatory fate in the Father's hands.

"A wonderful suggestion," said I enthusiastically.

"Nothing v-very extravagant, gentlemen," Mendel added apologetically as he waived the waiter over. "I live modestly, in observance of the Rule of St. Augustine.

"Let's see," he directed to the waiter, "we'll have a platter of Prague ham, some smoked tongue, a little of that Russian crab meat in mayonnaise, eggs with caviar. And oh, mounds and mounds of pickles." The little friar proceeded through a staggering list of delicacies.

I could not help but notice a devilish expression of curiosity on Holmes' face and anticipated his question.

"With all respect, Father, does a mendicant friar dine this well…every day?"

"Oh no, Mr. Holmes," Mendel quickly replied, laughing and slightly embarrassed at the pointedness of Holmes' inquiry. "I do live quietly and very modestly. But to-day," he continued, smacking his lips, "I indulge."

The first course was delivered to our table. Holmes had just lifted his fork when Father Mendel reverently bowed his head. With a toss of eyes toward the heavens, my friend furtively returned the utensil to its place on the tablecloth while Mendel began muttering grace. Then we toasted *"Na zdravi!"* with mugs of icy Urquell beer and proceeded to savour Lucullan portions of well-boiled meat in thick gravy, accompanied by large dumplings.

I was enjoying my meal when I noticed that Father Mendel's eyes had taken on a vacant, other-worldly look once again. To my surprise, his gaze appeared to point in the direction of my platter. By the expression on Holmes' face, he shared my observation. Imagine my alarm to detect the Father whispering under his breath, "My children."

With an astonishment on Holmes' face that I have rarely observed, he implored, "Forgive me?"

Mendel slowly placed his silver down as a blush spread across his face. "Gentlemen, you m-must think me o-odd in the extreme."

The expression on Holmes' face transformed into an amalgam of quizzical amusement and deepening interest in the Father's extraordinary behavior.

"Is there something troubling you, then?" I probed with heightened trepidation. Yet another flush passed across the Father's face as he cleared his throat and shifted his gaze from the platter to me.

"I was admiring…your peas," declared Mendel.

"My what?" I blurted out, rather impolitely in hind-sight.

"Your peas. The peas on your plate. They are," and with these words he chuckled oddly, "my children."

With the remarkable disclosure, I noticed Holmes' growing interest in Mendel's demeanor, so much so that my companion leaned forward so as not to miss the slightest intonation in the Father's voice.

"Would you…care to explain?" I asked, attempting an air of indifference.

With quiet intensity, the Father began, "I have always had an inquisitive nature, gentlemen. Some years ago I conducted certain experiments with peas in my garden at the Monastery. Of particular interest to me were their individual differences. Some of the peas were large, some rounder than others. Some, though, were wrinkled. These, I felt, were the orphaned, the unwanted, you see, and I came to feel a special fondness for them, and in a sense, adopted them as m-my own."

With a certain relief, Holmes and I sank back in our chairs on hearing this disclosure from the Father.

"What was the nature of these experiments?" inquired Holmes. "I have been known to conduct a few of my own."

"M-Mine, Mr. Holmes, involved a search for the mechanism of heredity. Are you familiar with the term 'throw-back?'"

"Referring to the phenomenon of atavism, I believe, where a feature peculiar to a certain family's past may suddenly and mysteriously reappear, such as a birth-mark or a singular shade of hair or of eye colour. It struck me as an interesting area of study, perhaps of use in some professional area, but admittedly I could make little of it. Take my word, Father; for Sherlock Holmes that is an extraordinary admission."

"You are correct, Mr. Holmes. The phenomenon is puzzling. Nature does not easily give up her secrets, which is why I turned to my peas. I could grow them selectively, taking careful note of distinctive features, in the hope of finding the key to one of Nature's most intriguing puzzles, the rules of heredity."

"I commend you for your extraordinary attention to detail, Father," exclaimed Holmes. "For me, it would have been akin to torture to have applied the patience necessary to conduct experiments such as yours, rather like the sobriety of mind required to raise a child, I suppose, nurture a rose garden—"

"Or keep bees," I added. "Filthy habit."

"Thank you, M-Mr. Holmes, for those words. Luckily, life in the monastery allowed me the time, and with God's grace I found the patience to embark on my experiments. I believed then, as I still believe, that something within the germ c-cell transfers an essence from one generation to the next, skipping generations at times. I have discovered that this mechanism obeys simple natural laws."

"Your theory," I said, "strikes me as most ambitious, Father. Has our science progressed so that we may delve this deeply into Nature's mysteries?"

"For me, it has been a m-m-matter of observation and analysis. I have needed little else in the way of scientific equipment to answer my most immediate questions. To seek further, I think, would require lenses and instruments of a sophistication that I should find difficult to even imagine, let alone procure."

"But are you truly satisfied with the knowledge you have gained so far?" I pressed, slightly indignant with the Father's seemingly limited vision. "Is there truly a limit to one's inquisitive nature?"

"May this not be blasphemous to say, but one answer cries out: No! Over the years, I have written my own thoughts on just such speculation, gentlemen, musing to myself as to where the next generations of explorers in my field may take us. One thing is certain, a f-farther ranging mathematical system shall be needed, something far beyond Gauss' method of least squares: New powers to see d-d-deeper into the heart of matter: To go b-beyond numbers and charts and primitive observations by eye."

"What *would* you give for such a chance?" asked Holmes.

"Gentlemen, I should…I should sell my soul. God forgive me, but I should."

For a moment Holmes and I sat in silence following Mendel's startling, nay, blasphemous, confession.

"Did you not publish?" I asked.

A dark cloud settled over Mendel's face, and I noted his hands clenched with emotion.

"Oh yes, I made two disclosures, to the Brünn Society of Natural Sciences, in p-particular. But after my presentation, not one question was asked, gentlemen, not one.

"I felt humiliated. No one seemed to grasp what I was proposing, and with time I came to doubt m-my ideas myself. I abandoned my experiments, set aside my notes for future publication, God willing, and left my beloved peas to grow undisturbed in their garden." With a sigh, he added, "Perhaps my colleagues were correct in ignoring my work."

"And perhaps not," I suggested.

"You're very kind," said Father Mendel. Ordering a local champagne to accompany a basket of fresh fruit for dessert, Mendel added, "You must allow me to show you Brünn, gentlemen. We may dine at my home, and then, refreshed, you may continue your journey in the morning. Perhaps you could stop a few miles north at the grottos of Macocha and Sloup where you and your friend may go boating in underground rivers."

At that moment Holmes and I shared the same thought, exchanged glances and erupted in laughter.

"Excuse us," I attempted to explain, "a private jest, Father. You see, we were warned by a most charming but bizarre little man back in Vienna to stay clear of 'underground waters.' They were his very words."

"I wish we could accept the whole of your invitation," said Holmes. I sensed a tone of concern in his voice as he added the false constraint, "Watson and I have rather a full itinerary, but dinner would be most welcome."

The little man's warning came to mind, again, but I had never known Holmes to be superstitious or to give the slightest credence to the mystical arts. Having said that, I also knew Holmes to be an extraordinary mix of the Bohemian and of the scientist.

"Well, gentlemen," said Father Mendel, "this is a l-land of superstition and darkness, too. We have strange, serious customs at Christmas when evil spirits m-must be appeased, or so the peasants will have you believe. And then, we speak in whispers of the werewolf and of the vampire, the undead, in the Carpathians. Yes, if ever there were a land where a warning of disaster might be taken earnestly, it is certainly here."

With these words, we were sipping a last round of champagne in the jostling dining-car when I looked out the window. My whole body thrilled with foreboding at a striking sight in the great distance: The silhouette of an enormous beast, a wolf—or so I thought it a wolf—sitting high atop a bank of black-shadowed snow and baying under the silver moonlight.

CHAPTER 6

Theft at the Monastery

After we disembarked from our train, Holmes instructed a young man in buttons to send our luggage ahead to the hotel, freeing ourselves to accompany Father Mendel on a leisurely tour of Brünn that would eventually lead us to his monastery.

With the approach of twilight, I studied the distant span of a brooding fortification, a scab before the Moravian sky, whilst Father Mendel continued a running commentary of his beloved town.

"The Spielberg Castle, gentlemen," the Father said. "I have had the d-dubious honour of visiting its more inaccessible chambers." His arm swept across the panorama before us, patches of greens and lavenders in the dusk. "You see, Brünn rests on the eastern foothills of the Bohemian-Moravian Highlands, nestled b-between two hills, one behind us and this hill named after the Castle itself."

"I seem to recall," I interjected, "that an Italian poet...what was his name?"

"Silvio Pellico," added the Father, confidently.

"Ah, Silvio Pellico, yes...was incarcerated in its dungeons."

"And tortured, horribly tortured," added the Father gleefully. "Since the thirties Spielberg Castle has been a political prison, Dr. Watson. Many others, I fear, have shared Pellico's fate."

Moving our thoughts from that chilling account, Holmes and I took in more of the magnificent view before us, the cathedral of St. Peter on the lower hill, the palaces and the *landhaus* which Father Mendel pointed out, the narrow, crooked streets traversing the town and the sparkling Schwarzawa and Zwittawa rivers which nearly encircled the ancient town.

"And over there," the Father pointed to a distant Gothic structure, "that is my monastery, gentlemen. We should reach it by dark."

True to the Father's word, the sky was black and salted with shimmering stars when once we arrived at the monastery. A full moon painted a silvery tableau of the massive, lichen-blotched stone-work forming the Augustinian cathedral before us.

Passing through a series of great arches, we arrived at the entrance to Father Mendel's chambers when his door suddenly shot open from within, and a disreputable-looking figure dressed all in black—an animal-like, shocked expression on his sooted face—rose up before us. With a strength surprising for his slight build, the creature tossed Holmes aside, who had instinctively barred the villain's way. Gripping a portmanteau with a ragged shock of white papers thrusting out from one of its pockets, the blackguard tore past us to escape into the anonymity of night.

"My p-papers. My notes!" exclaimed Father Mendel, when we heard the neigh of a horse and the sound of a cab rumbling off at full speed.

"Quick, Watson," said Holmes with vigour.

Holmes and I ran to the Father's hansom and heard Mendel behind, crying, "Gentlemen, please, w-wait for me."

Mendel and I leapt into the cab with Holmes at the reins above us, and we were off with the clatter of hooves on cobblestone. I could hear Holmes lashing the horse on to greater and greater speed. Peering out, icy air stinging my eyes, I saw nothing yet of the fugitive coach. I looked up to see Holmes' nostrils flared with excitement. Back in the cab, I checked on the Father's welfare as he wiped his brow with a large kerchief.

"Are you all right?"

"I think so," he replied. "I'm just n-not used to such adventure. Worse, I don't understand what is happening."

We headed north, pitching and tossing wildly as Holmes pushed the horse on to overtake the fiend. I looked out again and in the distance, a black speck kicking up pepper-sized flecks of sod, was the blackguard's cab. The landscape grew strange and grotesque, the plant cover scanty with outcroppings of limestone ridges that seemed to glow in the moonlight.

We hurled ahead, the scenery becoming increasingly barren, desolate and wild. Rims of sinks, potholes and unroofed chasms etched in silver whipped by, and the ride grew ever more violent. I looked to the side, great chunks of sod and rock flying past with the ferocity of hooves at full gallop. I turned to Father Mendel to see him forming the sign of the cross in mid-air, his eyes shut tight in fear.

Ahead the run-away cab gained in size, and noting the wobble of its wheels with the violence of the ride, I began to fear seriously for its safety and for ours. The ground became unmanageable and the view fiercer still with deep, steep-sided, canyon-like gorges, gaping fissures and crags.

I looked up again at Holmes, his eyes slits afire with the thrill of the chase. At that moment I heard a great crunch ahead and the rasping and grating of our hansom grinding to an abrupt and violent halt. The fleeing cab had caught a large sinkhole and snapped off a rear wheel. It careened to a stop, capsizing on its side, its horse whining horribly on the ground, a tortured mass of broken limb and twisted rigging.

"There!" shouted Holmes as Father Mendel and I jumped to the ground. I caught the black figure of our man scrambling away from the splintered remains of his cab, the grip still clutched in a fist, with Holmes trailing but a few meters behind. The calcified ground crunched and crumbled beneath my feet as I hurried along the limestone outcroppings and hollows, stumbling over ridges and tripping on vertical fissures, the old wound in my leg smarting fiercely.

I bolted over a crag just in time to see Holmes slap his hand on the figure's shoulder, only to be violently shaken off as the villain swiped Holmes with the purloined satchel, then threw it at him in the heat of defeat. Suddenly the brute disappeared with a horrific scream. When I finally reunited with Holmes, I saw that our mysterious foe had stumbled into the entrance of a deep, vertical shaft and was hanging by the bleeding finger-tips of one hand to crumbling limestone, his right hand outstretched to meet Holmes' offer of aid.

"Hold on," cried Holmes. "Hold—"

Limestone suddenly crumbled away and the fiend plummeted out of sight with a lingering, nightmarish shriek. We heard the report of a faint splash far below and the roaring fury of underground waters.

Father Mendel reached the tragic sight, traced the sign of the cross in mid-air and recited last rites in a low murmur, whilst Holmes and I, dazed and bone-weary, lay on the limestone ridge, peering in vain into the blackness of the terrible, bottomless shaft from which the rumble of deep, unseen running waters drifted up.

CHAPTER 7

A Holiday Cut Short

Holmes and I solemnly sat with Father Mendel, close to the licking flames of a massive fireplace within the Father's study, the three of us trying our best to cast off the chill of the night and the desperate, terrified expression in the stranger's face the moment the karst landscape swallowed him whole.

"My Lord, Holmes," I exclaimed, "I can smell the little metaphysicist's tainted breath this very moment, his eyes looking intensely into yours as he says, 'Do not, Herr Holmes, go near unseen waters. I am seeing much trouble, much danger. I beg of you.'"

"I remember those words, too," he solemnly said, "though the brunt of the danger seemed to have fallen on the blackguard. Still, I admit that our mysterious guest has brought me an intriguing puzzle. What do my methods reveal to you, Watson?"

"Your methods?" inquired Father Mendel, sitting up straight in his chair.

"I beg your pardon, Father," apologized Holmes. "I had made a promise to my friend that I should abstain from any professional dialogue during our trip, hence my neglect to inform you of my profession. But I would say our unexpected adventure has abruptly nullified that resolution. Wouldn't you agree, Watson?"

"Alas, I suppose our little adventure has released you of any such pledge to me."

Holmes leaned in toward Mendel to state matter-of-factly, "I am the world's only private consulting detective, Father."

"I'm afraid I do not understand."

"You see, Father," I attempted to explain, "when a mystery proves unfathomable to Scotland Yard, for example—agents call on Holmes and often from our sitting-room in Baker Street, he solves the matter."

"The problem, Father, is often merely a combination of false logic and even poorer observation," interjected Holmes.

"Tell him something extraordinary, then, Holmes!" I challenged.

Holmes expelled a great sigh, saying, "I rather doubt Father Mendel is in any mood for 'parlour-games.' I for one am not. However, I am curious as to whether any papers of yours have escaped your attention, Father."

"No, I checked the s-satchel; they appear to be here, Mr. Holmes, all of them," replied Mendel, dipping into the leather pocket and thumbing through the fouled sheets, adding, "…this t-time."

"Curious," Holmes remarked, "the way you put it."

"It is only that over the years I seem to have m-mislaid many of my notes. I have not been able to locate whole batches of them, in fact."

"Tragic," Holmes exclaimed, the hint of a smile playing upon his lips. "The missing documents: They are notes of your published work?"

"Funny, Mr. Holmes. Now that you mention it, *only* my personal notes seem to have disappeared, the unpublished musings I alluded to on the train."

"Do you consider yourself a forgetful man?"

"Why no, Mr. Holmes," replied Father Mendel thoughtfully.

"Curiouser and curiouser. Then it is fair to say that mislaying an item is unusual for you?"

"Yes, I pride myself on my m-memory, actually, if a Father may be permitted pride in one's accomplishments or personal habits."

"Then, when it comes to something as valuable as notes pertaining to your scientific pursuits, misplacing such items would be odd in the extreme. Is that fair to say?"

"Yes…oh, I see the direction your logic is taking us. But I can see nothing in such notes that a m-man should risk arrest and even the l-loss of his own life to obtain. This is what has me completely mystified."

"The inability to see the obvious," said Holmes, placing the tips of his fingers together and darting a sharp glance in my direction, "is a common foible, perhaps even a contagious affliction.

"But our evening must draw to a close, Father Mendel. Let me stress that you should not hesitate to inform me should further incidents occur; here is our address in London. I believe that some entity considers your work, however *outré*, of utmost importance, important enough to risk—if not his life—the life of an emissary."

Later in our hotel room, I could not help but notice Holmes as he absently massaged the arm in which he had so often injected the vile agent in times of duress or of simple boredom. Despite his facile explanation to Mendel of the events that had ensued, he seemed to be calculating a wealth of alternatives in his agile mind.

"These *are* deep waters, Watson, deep and unseen. I shall be very much surprised if Father Mendel does not contact us shortly upon our return home."

"Return home?"

"My profoundest apologies, Watson. We must hurry back. Something of extraordinary depth is occurring before my very eyes but so close that it has yet to come into focus. I haven't enough raw material with which to work, and I cannot make bricks—"

"Without straw."

"Yes, quite."

Silently, we drew in a few minutes more of the fire's warmth, then retired with the deepest fatigue of body and spirit. The cheery rays of morning sun, however, found me in a superior frame of mind, and I was heartened to see Holmes invigourated and eager to immerse himself in the growing mystery. Father Mendel was kind enough to see us off at the station from which we headed back to London.

To tell the truth I was becoming longful of reading *The Times* in my comfortable arm-chair in No. 221 B, Baker Street—a good mound of *Ship's* aglow in my pipe—and of looking across the room to Holmes, busy at one of his odoriferous scientific pursuits, test-tubes and flasks happily tinkling and bubbling away.

CHAPTER 8

A Lady in Distress

A solid London shower fell as Holmes and I walked our last few blocks from Charing Cross Station to Baker Street. Cabs slowed as they passed us by, but Holmes waved them on with his slight, almost feminine arm.

"A bracing walk, Watson," he said, "particularly in your good company."

"Thank you, Holmes."

"All the same," he added as we jumped a large puddle, "I find myself turning to something indefinable, bits of knowledge as yet unresolved all dimly floating in my mind, a most interesting and uncharacteristic experience for Sherlock Holmes. Watch out!"

He pulled me sharply aside as a four-wheeler tore past us, slapping a large wave of dun-coloured water in our path. Odd: Had I heard a coarse snigger coming from its cabin?

Ahead the statuesque figure of a woman seemed to be slowing its progress through the driving rain. From the manner in which her frame began swaying, I feared she was about to founder at any moment.

"Hurry, Holmes!" I exclaimed, pulling my friend forward by his coat-sleeve. "That woman is about to faint." We arrived at her side just as she collapsed by a stairway, her head missing by a mere inch the sharp marble edge of the first step.

Rain beaded on her fine features and soaked her garments as I checked her pulse. Despite my medical training, I found myself flushing as her clothing, heavy with their drink, left little to the imagination. Holmes scrutinized her, as well, but in that clinical manner to which I had become accustomed.

"I have her," I said, swinging her up and into my arms. For an instant, I imagined I held not this dark-haired stranger but my beauteous Lucy who had vanished so mysteriously from my life.

By good fortune, our rooms were only steps away, and soon Holmes was helping me lay the mysterious young woman gently upon the sofa in our sitting-room.

"Holmes, I must dry the young lady immediately. That means…that means I must—"

"Ah, I quite understand, Watson." Holmes' favourite dressing-gown suddenly appeared before my eyes. "If this should be of any use," he said, studying the young lady. "In the meantime, I shall have Mrs. Hudson find some suitable clothing for our guest and prepare hot tea."

Upon his return, Holmes set a very welcome fire blazing, and its cheery warmth began working its magic. Holmes and I now changed out of our wet clothes. Soon we were sitting in our respective chairs, shifted to face our still unconscious guest. Holmes studied the young lady in a silence broken only by the occasional pop and sizzle of the burning logs and by the scratch of his pen when he marked, I supposed, a thought of import on a slip of paper in his lap.

"Forgive me for entering your area of expertise, Watson, but the signs strike me as unmistakable. The pallour of her skin, the temperature of her body, the dark rings encircling her eyes and the marked degree of dehydration. Our guest fainted from sheer hunger. Would you concur?"

"Holmes, you are a constant source of surprise," I acknowledged. "Your knowledge of diagnostic technique is exceedingly impressive. Yes, I think that you have analyzed her condition quite accurately and completely. What this young woman most needs is solid nourishment: A diet of rich cream and butter, I would say, and rest, plenty of rest at this time."

"I have had the audacity to trespass into your arena," said Holmes, "with some remarks of a medical nature. In all fairness," he slyly continued, "I should enjoy having you enter my domain and share your thoughts as to the nature of our mysterious young lady."

"Very well, Holmes," I said, embracing his challenge. "In fact, I have been rehearsing your methods of late in the mundane, daily transactions of life. I find that, as with a muscle daily exerted, your methods attain a certain ease with use in no small while."

"Indeed? I am encouraged. Please continue, Watson."

"Firstly, I should say that the young lady is a maiden. Note that she bears no wedding band on her finger."

At this point, Holmes scratched a notation which I took to be an insight of mine that had struck him as particularly profound.

"Pray continue," begged Holmes. "I find your observations enlightening in the extreme."

Encouraged by his favourable comment, I was about to return to my analysis when our guest began to stir, her eyelids—rimmed by the longest lashes ever I had the privilege of viewing—fluttering erratically. She awoke momentarily and shifted slowly to a sitting position.

A frightened, bewildered expression appeared on her face as she explored the unfamiliar dressing-gown on her person and the strange room in which she had found herself. Happily, Mrs. Hudson appeared at the door, in her arms a tray brimming with sandwiches beside a large, steaming tea-pot.

"Excellent, Mrs. Hudson," I exclaimed. "In addition," I added with upraised finger, "I think the young lady may need something more substantial." I moved to the cabinet where I stored a crystal decanter sparkling with warm-coloured liqueur. It was the wonderful armagnac and unjustifiable extravagance that I had discovered as a medical student and included ever since among my vices. Alas, the decanter was nearly empty. For one instance I regretted my offer of these last precious dregs to the beautiful stranger, but with a shrug I accepted the trap into which I had placed myself and brought forward the amber treasure.

As I poured a stream of the deep golden liquid into a glass, I could not help but notice our guest's self-restraint against leaping upon the meal so close at hand.

"Please," I insisted, "drink this down and eat something."

"I'll see what I can do about finding some dry clothes for the young lady," said Mrs. Hudson. "Will there be anything else, Mr. Holmes, Dr. Watson?" she asked, her brow knitting with concern as her eyes trailed up and down the folds of the dressing-gown meagerly covering the young lady.

"Frankly, yes," exclaimed Holmes. "We shall need a great favour from you to-night, Mrs. Hudson. Would you be willing to put the young lady up for the night?"

Mrs. Hudson hesitated for a moment, then with a touch of suspicion in her voice, answered, "Anything for you, Mr. Holmes." Then she chuckled and added, "If I can put up with your tattooing Her Majesty's initials on my wall with your pistol…"

Her voice trailed off and as she turned to face the marks on the wall—a large V.R. shot in bullet pocks above the mantelpiece. I noted an expression of alarm registering upon the face of our guest.

"Send her down to me after her supper," Mrs. Hudson said as she approached the young lady. "Don't worry, Miss. You're in excellent hands." Mrs. Hudson placed the supper tray alongside our guest and left, but not before giving Holmes and me a quick, circumspect glance.

"Please, young lady," I implored, pointing to the tray, "please have something to eat."

Showing great restraint, she smiled weakly, slowly moved to her lips one of the sandwiches Mrs. Hudson had prepared and made a brave attempt to delicately nibble at the meal. In a moment, however, her restraint had dissolved, and she was now devouring the morsels with greedy abandon. After several more of Mrs. Hudson's delicious sandwiches and steaming cups of tea, she seemed to step back and look upon herself from afar at the pitiable state in which she found herself.

"I've made a complete fool of myself, haven't I?" she felt moved to say, a tear welling in her eye.

"Nonsense," I responded comfortingly. After she returned to sampling the sandwich in hand, only more demurely than a moment before, I cleared my throat and offered, "My name is Dr. John Watson, and this is my friend, Mr. Sherlock Holmes."

She looked up at me and then at Holmes, and I could have sworn that a small, special smile played upon her face. Holmes proffered the nod and brittle smile familiar to me and with which he believed he fulfilled any and all obligations of social propriety.

"Mr. Holmes and I have taken a liberty. You have gone without food for some time. Is this not so?" I queried.

She placed down the remainder of sandwich in her slender hand and poured herself another cup of tea. A moment of silence passed as she drew in strength from the steaming, invigourating brew.

"You're quite correct, Dr. Watson," she admitted with newly-restored strength of voice. "Let me see. I belicve that I last dined—if one may call it that—some three nights past with a tin of tongue I found in the corner of a cabinet. Oh, and a moldy peach for dessert." Her eyes lowered. "Thank you both for your kindness."

With these words, she buried her face in her hands and began weeping softly. Holmes offered his pocket kerchief in an uncharacteristic touch of gallantry, then swiftly returned to the comfortable distance of his arm-chair.

When she seemed to restore her composure, Holmes gently prodded, "Would you be so kind as to tell us precisely who you are?"

CHAPTER 9

Catherine de Quincey

The young woman who lay soaking in the icy London rain only an hour earlier—brought to a state of unconsciousness for lack of sustenance—now sat comfortably before Holmes and me, her back straight, a demeanor of composure and innate refinement.

Her face was classically oval with a complexion of creamy purity that I have only noted before in a few cameos of the finest quality. Her deep black hair—small ringlets forming where it was still slightly damp—shone with a soft brilliance in the light of the sitting-room lamps. A pear-shaped birthmark graced the base of her ivory neck.

"My name is Catherine de Quincey," she began in answer to Holmes' request, a musical, confident tone in her voice. "My family is from Lancashire Tarrant where I was raised in relative comfort. My father was a veterinarian before he retired. Much to the consternation of friends and family, I developed an interest in the same field.

"Despite conventional expectations from my family, I pursued an education toward that end. Roadblocks presented themselves at every turn. In the end no one supported my goals. However, I persevered, and then some seven months ago, I met a young gentleman from America. That is, I thought him a gentleman at the time.

"I gave my heart to him entirely, especially when he implored me to continue my plans for a career in the veterinary field, and his sentiments seemed wholly and selflessly in my behalf. We made plans to wed, and he swore that he would do all in his power to support my ambitions to become a professional woman.

"And so we married. All seemed so wonderful, as in a dream. But then what little I really knew of his character began to take shape. I discovered that at times he drank heavily," and then she cast her eyes down to the floor, "and one night I discovered to my horror that he even partook of vile drugs…cocaine, and worse."

Holmes shifted noticeably in his chair with these words.

"Then I discovered," she continued, "that gambling was his sole source of income which, till then, had been a point of mystery and of concern for me.

"When we met, he had been—as he would put it later—'on a roll.' But several months after our marriage, his luck had taken 'a turn' to use another of his expressions. As his gambling debts increased, he drank more heavily and began injecting the horrid drugs several times a day.

"One night, that he might pay gambling debts, he demanded savings of mine that I had set aside to further my education. Upon my refusal, he shook a fist in my face with further demands and threats, but I staunchly held my ground. And that is when he struck me across the face with the back of his hand, so hard that I fell back violently and grazed my head on the edge of the hearth."

"The beast!" I exclaimed. "Excuse the interruption. Please continue."

"Well, gentlemen, the violence of my fall seemed to restore some inmost grace, a newfound shame, in my husband. He gently helped me to my feet and then to our bed with a string of apologies, swearing to heaven that he would never strike me again from that night forth. Tears even came to his eyes, and he shuffled off like a lost soul to our sitting-room, plucking up along the way a decanter half-filled with whiskey and closing the bed-room door. I give him this; from that night on, he neither mentioned my savings nor lifted a hand against me.

"That same evening, though, I resolved to leave him within the month." Catherine de Quincey dabbed her eyes, moved by her own testimony. Then she threw back her head laughing and confided, "But he left me first, gentlemen.

"A fortnight ago, I came home to find our apartment gutted, all his possessions gone and most of mine, including what jewelry and fur-pieces I had collected over the years. In the morning, I discovered that our bank account had been drawn in full and closed.

"Since then I have been seeking employment as a typewritist, living on the few pounds in my possession the day he left. That money quickly vanished.

The food in the cup-boards ran out three days ago, and my landlady locked me out of my flat just last night."

"Good heavens, what a frightful predicament," I declared.

"Yes, the world can turn terribly cold in an instant. I found myself penniless, homeless, an outcast from the life of comfort I had always known and had taken so for granted." She drew us in with her coal-black eyes. "It's a sordid tale, gentlemen, I'm afraid, that I've brought you," she lamented with a sigh.

Holmes handed me the pad upon which he had been scribbling. I saw that he had enumerated virtually each point in the young lady's account and that he had been so brash as to check off each of his deductions as she confirmed them one by one in the telling of her story.

Holmes leaned forward from the soft, worn leather of his arm-chair. "Tell me, Mrs. de Quincey, was it Tuesday or Wednesday last when you pawned your wedding ring? I regret you received so little for it."

Catherine de Quincey's eyes widened in amazement. "I don't recall mentioning anything about a ring, Mr. Holmes."

"Mrs. de Quincey," I interjected with a chuckle, "you'll need to accustom yourself to Holmes' extraordinary powers. He can see right through you."

With this remark, she squirmed slightly in her chair and instinctively pulled at the hem of her garment. "Is it some kind of black magic, then?" she asked ingenuously.

"No, young lady," I reassured her. "Holmes is no sorcerer spilling lamb's blood on moonless nights, although I think himself as such at times. He has refined the act of deduction to an art. But by Jove, Holmes! How the deuce *did* you arrive at that bit of news?"

"Child's play," he exclaimed. "The third finger of your left hand, Mrs. de Quincey, bares a white ring of nearly translucent flesh. That tells me quite obviously that until recently you wore the wedding ring which you were forced by circumstance to surrender. Nearly invisible flecks of green within the band of white tell me that the ring that your husband gave you was of inferior quality. You, therefore, were recompensed little for it at the pawn shop, if I am not much mistaken, little more than for a day's provisions."

"The man is a miracle-worker!" she exclaimed, exhaling breath she had been holding in awe of Holmes' terrifying analytical powers. Even so, I could see that the young woman's energy was rapidly fading with the lateness of the hour and the stress of her strange surroundings and of her terrible disclosure.

"I think that the hour has come," I suggested, "to have our landlady fix you up in a comfortable bed." I led her downstairs, leaving the young woman in Mrs. Hudson's capable hands.

CHAPTER 10

A Plot Thickens

I awoke the following morning with Catherine de Quincey in my thoughts. Her determination and her story had made a deep impression upon me. I desired to improve her situation and resolved to enlist Holmes' aid on her behalf before the morning's end. Hot coffee and the first post were brought upstairs whilst I juggled several ideas about in my head.

"How is the young lady doing?" I asked as Mrs. Hudson set down the serving-tray on the side-table.

"Still soundly asleep, Dr. Watson. She was very tired last night, poor dear. We spoke only so long as it took to show her to her room and help her settle in. But I can tell you, she was most grateful for your kindness, yours and Mr. Holmes'."

"She said as much several times." And then Mrs. Hudson's eye-lids tightened a little. "You weren't thinking of asking me to knock her up, were you?"

"Not at all," I protested, "she may slumber away the day for all I care."

"Very good, Dr. Watson," Mrs. Hudson said with a concurring, motherly bob of her head. "Did you wish me to knock up Mr. Holmes?"

"No, Mrs. Hudson. Please, allow him to sleep just as late as he—"

Just then, Holmes swung open his bed-room door, saying, "That's terribly considerate of you, Watson, but up I am." In a moment, he was sinking into his comfortable arm-chair and reaching for the coffee.

"Allow me, Holmes." My hand beat his to the coffee pot, and I poured a steaming stream of the deep black brew into his cup.

"You are too kind," Holmes said dryly as he riffled through the bundle of papers Mrs. Hudson had placed on the side-table. He took a sip of the strong coffee and then lanced me with the piercing gaze of his slate-grey eyes. "You are *too* kind. You want something from me, Watson. Denial is of no use. Come clean."

"To you, I am as transparent as crystal, Holmes," I said with a sigh." I gathered my courage, deciding to state my thoughts plainly. "I have been thinking of the young lady."

"Which young lady? Lucy Gates?"

"Catherine. Catherine de Quincey."

"Why Watson, you are turning positively libertine as you mature," Holmes snidely remarked.

"I think you know very well what I mean, Holmes. I should like to help Mrs. de Quincey. Or rather, I should like *us* to help her."

"Well, well. You're exceedingly generous with my spirit of generosity," Holmes said sharply. "Is there an idea here somewhere?"

"Look round you, Holmes. There is much to organize."

"Where?" he asked, indifferent to the disarray distressing my sight.

"You have only to look round with those sharp eyes of yours, Holmes. Remarkable: How the acuity of your vision rises and falls with the topic of conversation."

"Watson, have you ever considered that one man's muddle might be another's index to some private world?"

"I'm well aware you have your own distinctive methods, Holmes…I…" I saw my campaign sinking dismally into the mire even as I continued speaking in Catherine de Quincey's behalf. I tried setting down my cup and saucer without the tell-tale rattle that would surely signal lost resolve to one as perceptive as Holmes. "Do you not wish," I continued doggedly, "to aid this young lady in her insecure situation?"

Holmes had begun thumbing through his morning correspondence. After a moment of silence, my companion muttered abstractly, "She may be worthy of some little assistance from you."

"Us!"

Very well. Us."

"Then, can you not open your heart a little more warmly to her? And can you not consider my suggestions a little more openly and a little more dispassionately?"

"Look here, Watson!" Holmes said with newfound vigour, shaking open a folded correspondence. "Something from our abbot. Ah, I thought as much would happen. 'Yet another attempt, Mr. Holmes,' he writes, 'this time halfway successful in that some of my notes were definitely pilfered. If any good may be said of the incident, it is that it happened during my absence'…and so forth."

"Holmes, you are not listening—"

"Halloa, and a note from Sir Charles! No less than three of them, in fact," Holmes now exclaimed.

"Sir Charles?"

"Charles Darwin, Watson."

"Impossible!" I scoffed.

"It is true, Watson. I have rendered Sir Charles some minor services, of little consequence, over the years."

"But Sir?"

"Ah, you are well informed, Watson. No, he has never been formally knighted, an unforgivable oversight. So, out of the deepest respect, I call him Sir Charles. He hates it, probably as much as I despise his calling me Sherlock. But you were saying something about…"

"Catherine de Quincey."

"Ah, Catherine de Quincey," he repeated, preoccupied with the content of the last of Darwin's missives. Holmes put the tips of his fingers together and bowed his head to his breast in concentration.

I heard Holmes mutter under his breath, "How one may undertake one woman in one's life, let alone two…"

"As to the young lady?" I pressed.

"Young lady…ah yes, your lady in distress…" he muttered. "Well, of course, you're right, you old lothario. Let us give her such aid as you deem appropriate."

I nearly leapt in the air with his words. "Holmes, you fill me with joy. But, what can we do?"

Holmes rose with Darwin's note clutched in his hand and began circling the sitting-room, the sash of his dressing-gown swinging violently to and fro with his nervous energy.

"I suppose there is much Mrs. de Quincey might do to aid us both," he ruminated absently.

"And in turn herself," I added.

"Your aspirations as a writer: Did she not say she had been looking for a position as a typewritist?"

"Typewriters, again, Holmes."

"Yes, by Jove. She should certainly be handy in aiding one of your lurid manuscripts to publication. And that hodge-podge of a desk of yours. Perfectly unseemly."

"It may be of inestimable help to have my many notes transcribed."

"You see? The very finger of fate writ broadly before you, my man."

"In fact, I recently carted a Reynolds typewriter up to my room. I intended to teach myself how to use the damned machine but could not get the hang of it."

"I agree, Watson,…typewriters, devilish contraptions," Holmes absently remarked, still studying his mail with intensity. "One day, some poor fool shall get his fingers all tangled up in that hideous labyrinth of metal and cables."

I slapped my thighs heartily. "Done, then! She shall be our personal—"

"I must send a message to Sir Charles by the next post!" Holmes exclaimed, closing his bed-room door behind him.

"—secretary."

With apparent consent from Holmes, the next and perhaps greater hurdle now presented itself: Catherine de Quincey, herself. I had resolved to employ her before even consulting the spirited young lady. As she relayed her story to us the previous night, I sensed a strong independence of nature just beneath the cool surface.

What should she think of my proposal? Would she accept my interest in the spirit in which it was offered. Or would she infer some ignominious intent behind my proposal? After all, she had so recently been wronged by her husband.

The opportunity to find answers to my questions quickly presented itself when I heard a firm knock on the door and Catherine de Quincey entered the sitting-room, cup and saucer in hand, an engaging smile upon her ivory face.

"Good-morning, Dr. Watson. It is a wonderful morning. May I join you?"

"Please do," I exclaimed, escorting her to the arm-chair close to the crackling log-fire. "Tell me, how do you feel?"

"Last night was the first peaceful sleep I had in days, thanks to your kindness and Mr. Holmes'. Is he not here?" she asked looking round.

"He is engaged at the moment."

"I see. I don't mind telling you that but for you and Mr. Holmes, I don't know where I should be at this moment." Her smile lit the room.

"More coffee?" I offered, lifting the inviting, gleaming pot to the lip of her cup.

"I should love some more, Dr. Watson. Thank you."

I poured her coffee as I pondered the delicacy of my upcoming proposal.

With a shrug, I exclaimed, "There is no way to begin but to start. Mrs. de Quincey, Holmes and I have been discussing your situation.

"Oh my, really?

"We are eager to help. Would you allow us to offer some aid and comfort?"

"What had you in mind?" she asked hesitantly.

"We should like you to accept our offer of a position, Mrs. de Quincey," I continued, nervously clearing my throat. "We should very much enjoy employing you as our personal secretary." To my delight, Catherine de Quincey's face brightened like a burst of fireworks with the invitation.

"Would you?"

"Mr. Holmes, you see, is the world's only private consulting detective," I explained. "And I have the honour not only of his friendship and companionship but of assisting him in certain of his more important cases. In our war against the criminal element, we are a formidable team. But in those more prosaic but vital skills demanded in day-to-day life, we admit to a certain inadequacy.

"I recall that you are a typewritist. I plan to chronicle Holmes' cases from time to time and should find your skills invaluable."

With a laugh and a lilting toss of her head, Catherine de Quincey said, "How can I decline such a delightful offer, Dr. Watson?"

"Then have we an understanding?" I asked.

"We have, sir, indeed!" she heartily exclaimed, warmly offering her hand. "But where do you suggest I stay?"

"I believe we may extend the arrangement begun last night. I shall discuss that with Mrs. Hudson later to-day. Would that be satisfactory with you?"

Lifting her coffee demurely to her lips, Catherine de Quincey said softly and mysteriously, "Quite."

CHAPTER 11

The Meddler

Returning from my constitutional the following morning, I found Holmes fervently protesting to himself, "This will not do!"

"What has provoked you so, Holmes?" I inquired.

"That woman."

"Catherine de Quincey?"

"She is The Meddler! I see that now. I meant to review Sir Charles' messages. They are gone, lost to the trash bin, I have no doubt. And look at this, Watson."

Holmes thrust one of his walking coats before me, turned out empty pockets and crossly tossed the garment on the floor. He repeated this ritual with two other garments and finally exclaimed, "Empty, Watson! No pencils, no slips of foolscap. And where are they? I discover them neatly—I repeat!—neatly stored within these damned China boxes. She has assassinated me, Watson, many times over!"

"Pencils? Paper, China boxes? What on earth is this all about, Holmes?"

He leapt to the mantelpiece, pointing to the worn, one-inch gash in the polished cherry-wood.

"My dagger, Watson. What has become of my treasured Macedonian dagger? Tell me that, will you! And the commonplace book excerpts I had pinned underneath?"

He marched indignantly to his bureau drawer.

"That was a rhetorical question, Watson; I shall tell you. The dagger is neatly—neatly, damn it all—stowed in its rightful place. And my excerpts are no more." Holmes landed a fist smartly on the desk top.

"Holmes, you do her wrong."

"Do her wrong?" he countered. "She has violated me, Watson!"

"Holmes, my dear fellow, you go too far, I cannot recall your ever being so unnerved. Do simmer down," I strongly advised.

"On your insistence, Watson, I agreed to employ this woman as a secretary, not as my surrogate mother! And where the devil is Catherine de Quincey, in the first place?"

I swallowed hard, muttering, "Flowers," in a hushed voice.

"Flowers?"

"She is gathering flowers. Brightens up the place, she said."

"Brightens-up-the-place." Holmes seethed now as he spat out each of these words with syrupy disdain. "This is the proverbial last straw!" he bellowed when the door swung open.

In stepped a radiant Catherine de Quincey, milky white skin glowing as only an Englishwoman glows with the crisp sting of morning air. Wildflowers cradled in her arms dappled the handsome face with pastel splashes as from the prismatic facets of stained-glass.

"Good-morning, gentlemen," she began brightly. Sensing tension in the air, she turned from one to the other of us as if to inquire what was had gone amiss.

"Mrs. de Quincey," challenged Holmes with scathing directness, "Mr. Darwin's messages to me are gone. My collection of commplace excerpts, my life's blood, are missing as well."

"The gentleman's posts were strewn on the floor like so much rubbish. Your excerpts—"

"—Did not the possibility of a gust of wind cross your mind?"

"Your excerpts were buried in dust, sir, and struck me as not of value."

"Not of value! By what right, young woman, do you turn my rooms upside-down?"

"I...I merely thought I should bring some order—"

"I find my dagger hidden in a drawer, my coat-pockets robbed of their contents, important missives gone, God only knows what other injuries to my person. Your duties, Mrs. de Quincey, are secretarial, not janitorial. The last thing they are is maternal."

"Forgive me," she said, obviously shaken, "I thought I was doing best. I have a theory, you see."

"Oh, you have a theory? Excellent. She has a theory, Watson! I am no longer the sole theorist of our household."

"Really, Holmes," I loudly protested, "you're behaving abominably."

"Yes, Mr. Holmes," Catherine de Quincey continued spiritedly, "I have a theory that tidiness in one's home fosters clear thinking, a quality I should have thought you would appreciate, given your profession."

"And Godliness," bellowed Holmes, "I dare say, is the topic of your upcoming lecture!"

A moment of awkward silence passed. The young lady solemnly placed the bouquet down on the table by her side.

"I see you're in no mood to discuss the matter, Mr. Holmes." She moved to the door, turned back to Holmes and asked rhetorically with a surprisingly effective mock inflection, "Beggin' yer pard'n, kind sir, but I 'ave been dismissed fer now, 'ave I not?" then firmly shut the door behind her.

Holmes moved to the mantelpiece where, it seemed to me, my companion tried losing himself in the play of licking flame. Then a deep sigh ushered from him as he shook his head.

"Am I that set in my ways, my boy?" he dispiritedly asked, clearing his throat.

"Hopelessly," I chuckled, "but then, I have always found your ways fascinating, Bohemian though they may be."

"You've a streak of the unconventional in you, yourself," he retorted with renewed pluck.

"Indeed. As do all the best people," I jested, managing to coax a grin from my companion. What say you to a proper English breakfast at the *Cafe des Artistes?*"

"I can think of nothing more restorative," Holmes responded. "On one condition."

"Yes, Holmes?"

"That I never…never…see that woman again."

With the clouds somewhat lifted, Mr. Sherlock Holmes and I left our rooms in Baker Street for a hearty repast, and my spirits were heightened in detecting a lilt returning to my companion's voice. If the display of passion I had just witnessed was typical of a woman's effect upon my friend, I better understood why Holmes took such pains to shun the fairer sex in his private life.

CHAPTER 12

Down House

Sherlock Holmes and Catherine de Quincey sat facing each other as the railway car sped on for Sydenham Station. Save for the gentle jostling of our cabin, the two could have been mistaken for waxworks worthy of exhibition in *Tussaud's*. More precisely, Holmes stared sternly and impassively past Catherine de Quincey. With soft but vacant eyes, she—by my side in our first-class cabin—stared past Holmes.

Even so, this macabre tableau was a tribute of sorts to whatever powers of negotiation I possess. Overnight, I had managed to convince my companion that Catherine de Quincey acted in the best of intentions and that her secretarial skills would be of practical use during our visit with Charles Darwin, if never again. And so we three now travelled under a tentative, fragile truce to meet with the great man at his estate in Kent.

Even in my relatively brief relationship with Holmes, I had come to understand that he enjoyed among his eclectic clientele those of great wealth, of celebrity and even of royal lineage. I remained nevertheless astonished to find that none other than Charles Darwin had left several urgent messages for Holmes whilst my friend and I had been *en vacance*.

Last night, my companion explained that the renowned scientist had come to rely intermittently on his astute faculties since the masterful detective had come to Darwin's aid in the interest concerning several earlier matters requiring a certain delicacy and discretion. Their brief but intense meetings hence and the brilliant results of Holmes' intellectual prowess had fused the fruits of their distinctive personalities into one, great abiding friendship built on the greatest mutual respect and admiration.

As we neared the station, amid icy silence, I reflected upon the immense intellectual talents of the gentleman whom I was soon to meet: A man who had broken the seal from Nature's Book of Secrets: Who had beheld the Grand Plan binding together the astounding variety of earth's flora and fauna with its myriad colours, forms, sizes and unlimited and subtle variation within each species. It all struck me as a Herculean accomplishment worthy of Darwin's ascent to the heady realm of the Pantheon. I eagerly anticipated making his acquaintance and what inquiries the gentleman's health and temperament should allow.

At last, the train lurched and pulled into Sydenham Station. We departed our cabin, and I secured a four-wheeler for our journey through the intense green of the Kent country-side, a splendid procession of rolling hill, dense woodland, bristling hedgerow and flower-specked field.

Catherine de Quincey sat by my side, the hint of a mysterious smile playing upon her lips. Across, Holmes had adopted a low slouching attitude in his seat. He was in fact in a dreamy, trance-like sleep, his eyes lightly shut against the dappled light streaming through the rattling cabin windows.

Catherine de Quincey looked my way. I could make nothing of the enigmatic distance in her slight smile, but I felt encumbered to utter something, however prosaic.

"Enjoying the ride, Mrs. de Quincey?"

"Intensely," she whispered, throwing a glance in Holmes' direction and putting a finger to her lips with such an affected, theatrical gesture, I gathered she would just as soon have let out the most raucous of shrieks for the impish pleasure of rousing my good comrade.

"Is this your friend's idea of companionship?" she whispered.

"Posh, you take things too personally," said I. "I have seen Holmes in this state many a time withdrawing, tortoise-like, into some inmost part of himself, cutting off all round him that he might refine that engine of analysis within his being."

"Then it does not matter what I say, does it?" the young woman declared. "Does he always offer you this quality of companionship in your travels together?"

"No," said I, slightly taken aback by the sting in her remark. "Come what may," I added defensively, "I always find it a pleasure to be in his company. When Holmes chooses, he can be quite entertaining."

"Perhaps it is my company, then, that afflicts him so," she proffered.

"Holmes is not an ordinary man. He does little in the customary way. In time you will come to understand this."

"I daresay, Dr. Watson," she replied enigmatically. "I daresay."

Our four-wheeler was now rumbling through the quaint little village of Down. To my left I spotted a cluster of thatched cottages, a carpenter's shop and a charming inn atop a bakery. We passed an enormous walnut tree at the junction of three narrow lanes, then rumbled on to Darwin's estate.

"Holmes!" I declared, giving his knee a firm tap. "We have arrived," upon which Holmes sprang to life with such animation that I started, banging the back of my head against the cab.

Our four-wheeler came upon a high wall of multi-coloured stone behind which Down House majestically rose. The driver followed a graveled path round the back, a great wooded area in the distance. Catherine de Quincey noted a distinctive sundial by the house where a gardener neatly clipped surrounding hedges. Finally, we dismounted the cab and approached the entrance beneath three stories of bow windows. My friend gave the massive front door's knocker a smart series of raps.

"I am Sherlock Holmes," he announced to the fresh-faced young maid answering the door with a dip of the knee. "My party and I have come at your master's request."

"Yes, sir, we've been expecting you."

She led us through a spacious hallway, our footfalls echoing in our ears, and into a cavernous, creme-coloured sitting-room. She disappeared by a side door as I marveled at a watercolour by Conrad Marten hanging from the facing wall, depicting the *Beagle* in rough seas, presumably on her way to the Islands of the Galápagos Archipelago.

At that moment, a strikingly handsome woman strode confidently through the doorway. Her commanding manner and appearance instantly proclaimed her as Emma Darwin.

"Gentlemen and dear lady, welcome to Down House," she said softly. "It is so good to see you again, Mr. Holmes."

"Always a pleasure," Holmes replied with warmth in his voice. After Holmes introduced Catherine de Quincey and me to the handsome woman standing before us, our gracious hostess gestured for us to sink into plush, velvet-lined chairs.

"I understand that my husband requested your presence again, Mr. Holmes, because of certain…preoccupations of his. Please bare in mind that Charles is very confused right now. As you know, he has suffered in health for many years. His constitution has weakened considerably since you saw him last. He is coming to doubt, I fear," and here she paused for a moment to contain herself, "his very mental faculties."

"Mrs. Darwin," Holmes said, "something weighty *is* on your husband's mind. I have complete confidence in his mental powers. However, one weak link in a chain of logic may lead one to some misguided conclusion. A distorted point of view may profoundly colour one's perception, not unlike cut crystal before one's eyes. I am here, Mrs. Darwin, as friend and counselor, to listen to your husband's concerns and to do my best to sort truth from conjecture, reality from prejudice."

"And I have accompanied Mr. Holmes," I added, "in my capacity as a physician who has encountered many strange diseases, Mrs. Darwin, particularly during my service in Afghanistan."

"So you served?"

"Oh yes, there's a Jezail round buried somewhere in this carcass of mine as proof. Be that as it may, I am a great admirer of your husband. I should be honoured to offer an opinion as to any medical influences that may be compounding your husband's distress."

I noticed pain in Emma Darwin's eyes as she nodded appreciatively to me; beneath her cool, gracious exterior I sensed unspoken burdens.

"Very well. Allow me to take you to Charles, now," she offered and led us from the sitting-room to a verandah, white lattice-work atop and appointed with simple wicker-chairs padded with bright red cushions. From there, we went round the house upon a fine gravel foot-path to a kitchen garden where we found Charles Darwin kneeling on the ground.

From his stance, it seemed to me that Darwin's gaze lay transfixed in the direction of a distant, deep-green hedge forming a high wall with an open entrance. To my utter surprise, I thought I saw standing there a vague human form: The figure of a man three-quarters hidden behind the hedge.

Emma Darwin tapped her husband gingerly on the shoulder of his loose-fitting black garment. "Charles, dear, your guests. I'll leave you to your business while I attend to lunch."

Darwin turned his massive head to us, his heavy-lidded, white-lashed eyes squinting in the sun and wrinkling the rubbery, simian face all the more. His wispy beard shot out from his face like white spray from the very seas he travelled so long ago in his youth.

"Sherlock, Sherlock!" he exclaimed in turning to my companion. But I was taken aback to hear the great man utter the bald fabrication, "I…was just observing a wondrous sight, Sherlock, playing out on the earth before me." I turned back to the hedge, but the shadowy form was now gone or hidden from view.

"Come close," Darwin demanded with feigned enthusiasm. "Observe." He pointed a thick, chalk-white finger at the soil, which shifted here and there by some subterranean force.

"Ah yes, you sent me a most intriguing paper on these worms of yours, did you not, Sir Charles?" Holmes exclaimed, extending his hand to help lift the great man to his feet and handing him a handsome, exceedingly heavy gnarled cane resting on the ground. "My colleague, Dr. John Watson. Watson, Charles Darwin."

"Yes, Sherlock told me much about you in his latest dispatch. Nothing good, I assure you," Darwin quipped with a wink.

"And my…" Holmes seemed barely to utter the words, "secretary, Catherine de Quincey."

"Delightful. How I envy you, Holmes. What a lucky man to have such beauty before you day after day after day."

"Yes, I often find myself wondering: whatever have I done to deserve this young woman," Holmes dryly agreed.

Darwin returned his attention to the turgid soil, now marveling with genuine admiration at the force beneath his feet. "Are they not a wonder, these worms of mine? Tillers of the earth, Sherlock!" he declared in a deep, resonant voice. "And as for wonders," he said turning in Holmes' direction, "how good it is to see you again. I remain forever in your debt."

"You make too much of my humble services, sir," Holmes gently protested.

"Be generous, Sherlock!" admonished Darwin. "Allow me to shower you with praise. Your aid in the past has meant more to me than you can ever know. And even though the stories still abound—about my stealing from Wallace—you quelled much of that storm." Clearing his throat, Darwin suggested, "Let's move to my study where we may all be more comfortable."

Charles Darwin escorted us back inside, through well-polished corridors and into a cozy study where the morning-fire still crackled, sending waves of warmth into the centre of the room. Books lay everywhere. Here and there a specimen jar glinted amongst other mysterious treasures: Weathered stones, powder mixtures, tins of chemicals.

Darwin set aside a beize-covered board resting on the arms of an enormous horsehair chair and fell deep in its confines with a great sigh of relief. He invited us to make ourselves comfortable when a roguish expression suddenly marked his craggy, deep-worn face. Putting a silencing finger to his lips, he rose furtively and gave a darting glance in either direction of the hall, then tiptoed to a stack of weathered books on a shelf, slid them aside and brought forward a small gilt box.

In anticipation we three tipped forward in our chairs. What wonder was the great man about to share with us? Darwin lifted the lid with all the ceremony of a child enacting some secret, mischievous rite and then gallantly offered Catherine de Quincey its contents: A selection of gilt-wrapped chocolates.

"Quick, young lady," he playfully snapped whilst Catherine de Quincey laughed at the stealth with which he had conducted his generous overture, "this is an unmentionable in my house."

As Holmes and I passed on Darwin's disappointing offer, his plump fingers brought a chocolate creme tremulously to his lips. A broad smile of satisfaction played upon his face as he re-buried the illicit hoard behind worn, leather-bound volumes of Lyell and Buffon. "You see how it is. Emma would prefer I take up opium smoking."

"You have our complete confidence, Sir Charles," whispered Holmes conspiratorially. Sinking back into his chair, Holmes pressed, "I am anxious to hear what has been troubling you, sir. Pray come to the heart of the matter."

"But of course," replied Darwin, lapping the last traces of cocoa butter from his fingers. "Mr. Sherlock Holmes," he continued, his deep-set eyes boring into my friend, "I am being poisoned."

CHAPTER 13

The Great Man's Dilemma

"Sir Charles," the gaunt detective pointedly said, "you have just made a startling claim. You think you are being poisoned. Has this suspicion to do with the physical ailments you have been suffering for so long?"

Darwin slowly nodded his head, great, shaggy white wisps of beard hanging feather-like in the air. "I am convinced of it," Darwin declared. "These maladies cannot be due to natural trauma."

"Please describe your symptoms to me, Mr. Darwin," I requested of the great man.

"A deep sense of fatigue, Doctor. Flatulence, insomnia, palpitations of the heart. My hands break out in small pustules. I am often nauseous, I frequently vomit."

"Have you tried the Water Treatment, sir?" I pursued.

Darwin laughed and shook his head despairingly. "Treatment on treatment at Malvern, Dr. Watson. I experienced short periods of relief but then more of the same." He shook, saying, "I can still feel those icy packs upon my stomach, those chilly foot baths morning and night."

"What of more desperate measures, Mr. Darwin, such as nitromuriatic acid?"

"The same results, Dr. Watson. Picture me, gentlemen—and young lady—my body trussed with coils of brass and zinc wire. Wet down with ill-smelling vinegar, transformed into a human battery in the hope that the electrical current thus produced should have some salutary effect." Darwin clenched his fist, and this he brought down sharply on the arm-rest. "No relief!" he boomed. "I tell you, Sherlock, I am being poisoned."

Catherine de Quincey cleared her throat in readying to offer a suggestion of her own. "Gentlemen…my training in the veterinary sciences may bring some light to the problem. Have you ever been bitten by mites, sir, parasites of some sort?"

"Bitten? During my travels I was nearly eaten alive by mosquitoes any number of occasions." Darwin then snapped his fingers with a particular recollection. "Halloa, there was one incident in Tierra del Fuego. I was attacked by an army of the most peculiar bugs. I never saw their like before or since. But it was years ago; that battle royale must have occurred back in the mid-thirties."

"It is my understanding," Catherine de Quincey continued, "that some insects carry parasites whose awful work may remain a mystery for some time, the damage only revealing itself years later in symptoms such as those you just described. Is that not so, Dr. Watson?"

"A bit out of my area of expertise, young lady, but yes, the indications may point to some parasitic condition."

Holmes gave Mrs. de Quincey a sharp glance of disapproval. "Who," he asked of Darwin as he found his pipe and traced its outline with deliberation, "should wish to poison you?"

"The Nine Unknown Men."

"Who are they?" I asked ingenuously.

"Who are the Nine Unknown Men?" Darwin echoed back, nearly laughing. "But no one knows. They're unknown. The Nine-Unknown-Men."

"Can you share nothing with us?" queried Holmes, impatience in his voice.

"How can I explain? They are a secret society, sworn to protect mankind from itself," Darwin replied.

"And what has a secret society to do with Charles Darwin?" Holmes prodded.

"They are…angry with me."

"Pray tell us more," pressed Holmes.

"They are an order out of ancient India, from what I understand. Initiated as a technological priesthood over 2,000 years ago, they wish to maintain their select status as 'keepers of the flame,' so to speak, the lone source of all scientific inquiry at all costs. Or so their letters suggest to me."

"Letters. From what you have said," reviewed Holmes, "the papers imply some threat of injury or retribution directed at you—"

"Quite, Sherlock."

"—Or at some member of the family. Your wife, for example."

"Emma! Would they be so vile as to harm my Emma?" exclaimed Darwin.

"I fear that is the implication," Holmes glumly replied.

"Their notes were not always so grave, Sherlock. At first, they were merely critical of my work. Well, I could as well have added them to a very high stack of correspondence stowed away somewhere. Over the years, the occasional delivery became a steady stream of threats, ever more demanding. Until now…"

"This strikes far deeper than we first thought," said Holmes. "For what deeds are they displeased with you?"

"Oh, they have made that quite clear in their little missives: For my life's work, sir. They see great danger in my having explored the mechanics of evolution. In their letters, they have denounced my publications as well as any speculation as to what the next generation of scientists in my field may reveal and how that knowledge should be put to use. They seem also to be aware of the general substance of my many unpublished notes, which they have demanded."

"Demanded?" I echoed with astonishment.

"Yes, they have decreed that I send them all my notes, every last one of them. And that they alone shall approve those studies deemed worthy of further investigation by me or by a fellow scientist."

"By all that's holy, I am dumbfounded!" I exclaimed. "Of all the audacious—"

"When did these messages begin, Sir Charles?" queried Holmes.

"Oh, some time ago, Sherlock. If I must put a date on it, I should say shortly after I first published my *Origin*."

"Why, that would be more than twenty years ago!" I said, my head spinning.

"Have you such correspondence at hand?" asked Holmes with excitement.

"Somewhere. I am not a very tidy man, gentlemen. If not for my Emma—"

"Please, Sir Charles," Holmes implored, "it is to our purpose. Shall we make an effort to find them?"

Darwin looked haplessly into Holmes' piercing eyes and forlornly shook his head. "I wouldn't know where to begin, Sherlock. I have probably thrown away as many letters as I have kept." Holmes and I exchanged knowing glances, the same thought in mind.

"With your permission," Holmes said, reaching impulsively under Darwin's massive desk to retrieve a waste-basket whose contents he was now briskly spilling onto the floor. Taking our cue, Mrs. de Quincey and I joined Holmes in rummaging through the debris.

"Halloa!" exclaimed Holmes, cocking his head whilst uncrumpling a ball of correspondence with anticipation.

He flattened the crumpled mass on the desk top with the palm of his hand and set to reading the message to himself. "Delightful," he dryly said. "Whoever wrote this missive means to enjoy being the sole repository of all knowledge, that's clear enough. Listen, Watson, to the demand.

"'You shall collect all records, data, notes, personal reflections, all originals and all facsimiles of all your scientific inquiry unpublished to date.

"'You shall send a telegram with the words, "The sky has many clouds," to the address specified below. In two days time a representative shall appear at your door at precisely seven forty-five in the morning. You shall hand him all the materials demanded of you.

"'This method shall save all considerable grief. Ignoring this message…'" Holmes paused dramatically, "'—shall result in serious consequences.'"

"How in Heaven's name," I cried, "can anyone display such unmitigated gall?"

"The question for now," Holmes asked pointedly, "is *who sent this message?*"

"But I have told you, Sherlock," Darwin replied with some little irritation in his voice. "The Nine Unknown Men!"

"I think not," he countered, holding the crumpled paper to the light. "This letter has never seen India."

"But surely, Holmes," I contended, "these Unknown Men wrote the letter in India, and an agent sent it from elsewhere, possibly from London, herself."

"A point, Watson, but one measured against a host of others indicating a different conclusion. Aside from qualities of the paper, itself, when you inspect the missive in total, the very phrasing gives the fraud away. However well educated a Hindoo may be, his speech and writing will reflect the timeless influence of his mother culture. I do not see any indications in this document. You need only look at the use of idiom, denotation and connotation, the absence of dialectal words. No, there is no question, this slip of paper may just as well have a pair of lips and a tongue, for it speaks volumes to me."

"Why should anyone care to go to such lengths to obtain Mr. Darwin's documents?" asked Mrs. de Quincey.

"Why, indeed. If these letters with their rather bald threats had persuaded Sir Charles to yield to the demands, how much easier to plunder the riches of his genius by that method rather than to come blundering in here under the darkness of night, blindly rummaging through his effects at the risk of disclosure or, worse, capture and possible imprisonment. Even you, Sir Charles, admitted the challenge of finding one document amid, excuse me for saying so, the clutter. But now we are ready for another question," continued Holmes, pressing the tips of his fingers together. "Has anyone attempted to break in, Sir Charles?"

"Not to my knowledge."

"Then you are not missing any documents?"

"I didn't say that, Sherlock. Over the years, yes, quite a few, even my beloved M and N notebooks."

"M and N notebooks?," I inquired.

"I have always kept private notebooks, Doctor. These two contained ruminations on transmutation, essentially the emergence or metamorphosis, if you will, of one species, a new species, from another."

Holmes' brows deepened. "Again, vanishing manuscripts, eh, Watson? And then this bizarre, protracted effort to attain the bounty in full. And yet another link, pointing to the primary nature of life as revealed by Mendel."

"Mendel?" repeated Darwin.

"Yes, Sir Charles," replied Holmes. "We recently made the acquaintance of an Augustinian monk, one Gregor Mendel, who has conducted research into the nature of heredity. You should find his work quite interesting. He, too, has suffered the theft of several manuscripts."

"You don't say, Sherlock. Fascinating, I must meet the gentleman one day."

"Sir Charles," Holmes inquired, "is your entire staff present to-day?"

"All but for one of the upstairs maids who is ill," replied Darwin.

"And among the staff, are there any of Indian descent?"

"Two, one from a village near Allahabad in the North-west Provinces, the other from…hmmm, I cannot recall."

"I should like to have the entire staff assembled immediately," demanded Holmes.

Darwin cooperated unquestioningly and in a few minutes the servants were aligned in one long row in the great hall of Down House. They darted quick, nervous glances at each other, questioning expressions upon their faces.

A stony mask upon his countenance, Holmes stood before the line of domestic and livery help and bore each in turn straight into the eye with his icy, grey-green pupils, allowed an uncomfortable moment of silence to pass, then deliberately removed the crumpled paper he had hidden in his coat pocket and held it above his head before the gathering. He moved to one end of the line, the paper still held high in the air, and slowly passed each individual member of the staff, pausing slightly from one to the other whilst giving the slip of paper a little shake of the wrist.

By the time Holmes reached the end of the line, not one of the staff had elicited a response to his intense scrutiny. With furrowed brow, he turned sharply on his heel and repeated the inspection of each of the servants' features.

Suddenly, one of the maids, a lithe, mahogany-coloured Hindoo turned deathly pale and fell to her knees, sobbing and exclaiming, "I beg you, Sahib, pity me." She looked up at the paper in Holmes' hand and then at Darwin with red, imploring eyes. With defiance in her breaking voice, she continued, "If this be my last hour in your service, so be it then, Sahib."

Darwin angrily snatched the document from Holmes and thrust it before the maid's eyes, brusquely querying, "Then it is *you* who is responsible for this?"

"I cannot read what is upon that paper, Sahib, but it must be about my referral."

"Referral?" echoed Darwin, taken aback.

"I needed a position so terribly. Can it be so wrong to have a friend—I shall not say the name, no matter the cost—to have someone make up such a paper that I might gain a position so to feed my children and not to have them starve and waste away as those in my country that are named the Untouchables?"

"Are you finished, Sherlock?" asked Darwin of Holmes. "Yes? Return to your duties," Darwin commanded of the rest of the assemblage. The young maid still lay on the deep carpet, her palms pressed to her tearful eyes.

"Sir Charles?" Holmes put to Darwin as if to ask what should be done with the young woman.

Darwin moved to the maid and offered his hand, saying with great tenderness, "Do not distress yourself, child. You acted on womanhood's noblest impulse. There shall be a place for you at Down House as long as you wish." With a profusion of gratitude, the young woman pressed her cheek to Darwin's hand, then disappeared down the hall.

"Sir Charles," Holmes said, "I do not believe any of your household has betrayed you. I never did, but I had to prove it to you with this sad demonstration. Nothing else would do. Neither do I believe that you are being poisoned. The threats and the disappearances of documents come from some external source hungry for knowledge, not for good but for some evil intent."

Darwin's eyes stared blankly into space. "When you think upon it, Sherlock," his voice now drained and distant, "all that I have said seems very peculiar, doesn't it?"

He moved unsteadily to slide aside the volumes protecting his sugary treasure. Leathery fingers mounted another illicit sweet to the lips but Darwin seemed numb to its pleasure now.

"I am sorry that I have wasted your time, Sherlock," he muttered weakly.

"To the contrary, Sir Charles!" Holmes exclaimed, rushing to his side. "You merely—"

"—870 tons," Darwin whispered, oblivious to Holmes' words. Then suddenly he clutched at his chest and swayed, his face contorted in pain, turning nearly translucent as blood drained from his flesh. Holmes rushed to my aid in carrying the great man to the soft embrace of a well-worn leather sofa. In a moment, Darwin gestured with his hand as if to say that all was well.

"Perhaps, the excitement of the morning has worn me down, my friends. I'll be fine after some rest, please do not worry." He turned to Catherine de Quincey who stood close by in a state of visible concern. "You're a very beautiful young lady."

"Ah," I exclaimed, "you *are* feeling better?"

"Well enough to flirt a bit behind my Emma's back," Darwin replied flippantly. But the forced smile quickly vanished and a darkly pensive Charles Darwin now met my gaze. "Please, go now," he insisted, "return safely to London and do not concern yourselves with the ravings of a sick, old man."

Darwin waved us off good-naturedly, and we left him resting peacefully on the sofa but not before Holmes bent to the great man's ear, whispering, "Consider this case in the hands of Sherlock Holmes. One thing more. Who was the man behind the hedge?"

"Man? What man?" Darwin protested innocently.

"Come now. The man you fixed upon so earnestly from the garden."

"You don't miss a thing, Sherlock. My shadow," Darwin conceded, after a pause. "He is always there. Or seems to be."

"Have you any notion who he is?" Holmes pressed.

"He is a distant, vague form, Sherlock. Damn it, man, I'm old. I cannot see clearly. I don't think I could ever see that clearly." Darwin's hand moved to his chest again.

"Very well," relented Holmes, resting his hand reassuringly on Darwin's massive shoulder. "Rest now."

"Holmes," I asked as we exited the sitting-room, "his statement, '870 tons,' do you suppose it is a vital clue to this mystery?"

"I doubt it."

"But the words sound so cryptic to me, Holmes, so full of mystery and promise."

"The volume of soil worms till in a year, Watson, nothing more. The figure is mentioned in one of his papers."

Emma Darwin found us readying to exit from the main hall. She could not persuade us to stay for lunch, but we assured her that we were at Darwin's disposal day and night. Holmes especially urged her to contact him by wire in the event of any new development or of heightened agitation on her husband's part.

We bade her *adieu* and mounted our cab for our return to Sydenham Station. Succumbing to sleep's call within the rocking frame of the four-wheeler, I found myself greatly dissatisfied with the results of our morning's work, a vagueness of purpose, unarticulated feelings and fears, ill-defined suspicions and shadowy, faceless foes haunting my thoughts. Then through fairy-land's delicately filigreed gates, Lucy—the young lady with the missing machine—lightly stepped upon my dream-stage and for too short a time, caressed away the troubled niches of my mind.

CHAPTER 14

Tommy

Catherine de Quincey, Holmes and I stood in Sydenham Station waiting for our late train to appear, an icy gale whipping through the cavernous structure and chilling my exposed face and hands to the bone. Catherine and Holmes had wisely brought gloves; mine lay forgotten in their cozy drawer in Baker Street. To allay my discomfort, I purchased an edition of *The London Times* from a sooty-faced news-boy looking far older than his years.

"Thanks, gov," he had the rough grace to exclaim when I handed him an extra coin. As I turned the leaves, my eye snapped to a familiar name in the sea of text.

"My word, Holmes," I declared, "listen to this." Just then, a whistle met our ears and we turned to see our delinquent train puffing into view.

"Can your recitation wait, Watson? The train is—"

"I think you'll want to hear this, Holmes. 'The police reported a bizarre incident last night in the East End near St. Paul's. A young lad of 12 by the name of *Tommy*—'"

"Tommy!" exclaimed Holmes.

"One of your—what do you call them—irregulars?" asked Catherine de Quincey of Holmes.

"Read on, Watson," Holmes hotly demanded, ignoring the young woman's inquiry.

"—bizarre incident…near St. Paul's…young lad by the name of Tommy was rushed to St. Bartholomew's—"

Suddenly, a stiff gust of wind ripped the paper from my hands, scattering individual pages into the air. The timing could not have been worse, for the train had just pulled up to us with an issue of dense, white billows of steam. What a comic figure I must have struck, groping through the thick mist whilst Holmes and Catherine mounted the train and rallied me on from the foot of its steps. I snatched what pages I could through the dissipating steam, hurriedly gathering them to my breast.

"Quick Watson!" shouted Holmes. "It's late enough. The train is pulling out."

I whipped up another couple of pages, then sped to the moving portal where Holmes and Catherine de Quincey stood with arms extended. With their aid, I swung my body into the warmth of the carriage's interior.

"Proceed!" Holmes commanded as soon as we entered our compartment.

I lay the crumpled pages before me, my eyes eagerly scanning for a familiar phrase.

"Ah," I continued, "we're in luck…'was rushed to St. Bartholomew's… where constables could get little information from the semi-comatose young man but his first name and very sketchy details of the occurrence. Eyewitnesses "of questionable repute" at the scene claimed that the boy and a group of his friends had been up to some mischief when they were suddenly attacked by some kind of beast in the dead of night. The boy's friends apparently managed to flee to safety, but Tommy was discovered laying in the street in a pool of his own blood by a sergeant who ministered as best he could a severe wound to the upper thigh till an ambulance arrived.

"'Said the constable, "If I wouldn't have known better, I'd have sworn it was a shark bite. Saw many of them during my stint in her Majesty's fleet when I was a lad myself."

"'An idler at the scene, one Luther Squibbs, was heard muttering that "monsters was loose on the land as prophesized in the Good Book," that he had seen them that very night and that the "end of the world was near." He was promptly arrested for public drunkenness.

"'The authorities are making further inquiries into the matter and request us to note that any assistance or additional eyewitness reports from the public would be greatly appreciated. Because of the threat to the public health, Inspector Lestrade of Scotland Yard has been placed in charge of the case and may be contacted day or night at his office.'"

"What a ghastly business, Watson. I must see the boy as soon as we arrive."

"Was he working on a case for you, Mr. Holmes?" asked Mrs. de Quincey.

"Yes, the disappearance of...that is of no consequence to you, young lady."

After a few moments of tense silence, we settled down for the remainder of our journey and none too soon were standing over little Tommy, his face scoured cleaner than I had ever witnessed. He was mumbling to himself, not yet conscious of our presence as we gazed upon him resting in the stark hospital bed.

Bending to the boy's ear, Holmes whispered, "Tommy, can you hear me, lad?"

Tommy lay unresponsive to Holmes' entreaty. Only nonsensical fragments flowed from the boy's lips.

"Beau'iful, so beau'iful...no, no, I shouldn't go no further...cats, so many cats...an' the chandelier, sparklin' like the sun...the eyes, the red eyes all around, make 'em go 'way...'"

Mrs. de Quincey patted Tommy's face dry and gently stroked his long, flaxen hair.

"...so many cats...an' the crystal...the eyes, all 'round, go 'way...'"

"I think we'll get little from the boy to-night, Holmes," I offered. "We'd best let him rest peacefully."

"Before we go, I must see the wound," declared Holmes.

"So must I," I added.

"And I," echoed the young lady.

"Are you sure you care to see this, Mrs. de Quincey?" Holmes asked.

"You forget, Mr. Holmes," she replied sharply, "I am a student of the veterinary sciences. I have no problem with the sight of blood, if that is what you mean to suggest."

"Excellent. Watson, begin the inspection."

I lowered the coarse, tan-coloured blanket hiding Tommy's extremities. The boy's right limb lay hidden under thick layers of gauze, stained ruddy-brown from huge blotches of blood. At the mere touch of my hand to the bandage, Tommy—even in sleep—groaned and thrashed his head to and fro.

"What's going on here?" a voice suddenly inquired. We turned to find a rather plump nurse standing by the door.

"I am the boy's physician," I replied.

"And I suppose you're the boy's rich uncle," the nurse testily countered, addressing Holmes, "come to check on your heir's well-being."

"None of that, now," I snapped. "I am John Watson and a medical doctor practicing here in London. This lad is in immediate need of a change of dressing. By the look of things, it should have been taken care of some time ago. I require fresh bandages and—"

"Now, look here!" the nurse protested.

"*And* a pair of scissors. Or must I make some inquiries to your superior?"

"No, no sir, I'll give you no trouble," yielded the nurse, leaving the room to return swiftly with the fresh dressing and instrument I had demanded.

As gently as I could, I slipped the blade of the scissors under the crusted layers of gauze and snipped away, slowly revealing Tommy's ravaged limb, splotched black and blue and a hideous jaundice-yellow from its trauma. Despite my years of practice, as I lifted the last layers of compress I could not help but hiss through my teeth at the sight of the ragged, foot-sized oval cavity excised from the boy's thigh. Catherine de Quincey turned pale and stepped back into a corner of the room, and I noted that even Holmes winced with alarm at the sight.

"My Lord, Holmes, what in heaven's name!"

"We must see the site where this horror occurred, Watson. Mrs. de Quincey, consider your day done."

"Yes, Mr. Holmes," Catherine de Quincey concurred, visibly shaken by the sight. "I have seen enough."

Back on the street, Holmes flagged down a hansom for the young woman and another for us two. The cab left Holmes and me on old Badley where ruddy patches still marked the pavement where Tommy had been attacked. I could see that days of foot traffic had erased much of the clarity of the message on the road that Holmes was even now attempting to decipher. He whipped out his glass and bent low on all fours, crisscrossing the area in an ever-widening arc. Suddenly, he pointed southward to a grimy entrance that led to the city's sewers beneath our feet.

We scrambled down into bleak, damp, slippery stone. Holmes ignited a portable lamp that he was in the habit of carrying on his person and with the pulsing yellow flame perused the unwholesome environment in which we found ourselves. We stumbled on in the darkness until something suddenly crunched beneath my boots. I stepped back, and Holmes swung the light near. Our brows rose in horrified surprise as we viewed the scene by my boot.

A scattering of small, delicate bones lay exposed in a shallow pool of black water. They were the remains of a child. A wooden doll splintered and pocked with countless marks tossed to and fro among the jumble of skeletal remains and shredded patches of cloth. Holmes walked on a few paces, swinging the beam of his lamp back and forth, then returned to the sorry remains of the youth we had known solely by a common, Christian name: Laura.

"I did say she'd turn up, didn't I?" Holmes uttered solemnly. "Nothing else is to be done here."

The following day I saw nothing of Mr. Sherlock Holmes—as was so often the case once he immersed himself in the minutiae of a case—until the evening hour approached nine o'clock when he burst through the door of our sitting-room. A look of gleeful mischief beamed upon his face, and he rubbed his hands in celebratory exultation.

"Watson," he exclaimed, pulling off his Mackintosh, "if ever you doubted my genius, I must pass on what has transpired!"

"I am all anticipation," I eagerly responded.

"Last night, Watson, I became determined to interview this witness, this Luther Squibbs, the hapless fellow babbling about monsters prowling London's seamy under-belly. The day started badly, though. I first discovered that the reporter who had written the article concerning Tommy's attack was just this morning sent out of the country on assignment. Despite my better judgment, I then paid a visit to our inestimable colleague, Mr. Lestrade, who—not surprisingly—was of infinite uselessness. He hardly turned his…how do you describe his eyes in those drafts of yours that you have allowed me to peruse?"

"Ferret-like?" I offered.

"Ah, Watson," Holmes continued, "you *do* have a gift for the descriptive. Yes, Lestrade hardly looked my way with those ferret-like eyes of his as I pressed for anything resembling data concerning our man. Neither he nor his associates had bothered to record a whit of pertinent information concerning Squibbs, not even a physical description of the fellow. Even Gregson let me down, except for sharing one solitary but significant tidbit: That the gentleman in question had been known to frequent Spitalfields."

"That god-forsaken area of Whitechapel?"

"Quite. I then made two assumptions, Watson: That Squibbs was bereft of a permanent abode—not highly speculative, I admit—and that even one as destitute as he would check the post in hope of the occasional handout from a family member or a friend. With no description to go on, I hit upon a brilliant idea, Watson! From a vendor in Covent Garden I purchased the largest wicker-basket I could find, filled it to brimming with fruit and, as a finishing touch, secured the handles with a very large and very vulgar bright yellow satin bow.

This I then left till called for by our man at the receiving station of the Whitechapel Post-Office.

"From then on, it was merely a matter of instructing Peter and little James of our unofficial force to take turns watching for the basket and the gentleman to whom it was attached whilst I attended to other matters. Ha!" Holmes suddenly exclaimed when Mrs. Hudson's decisive knock rang out from the door, "if I am not much mistaken, that would be our partner in crime come to report."

A Lilliputian ragamuffin shuffled forward after a gentle nudge from our good landlady who announced, "Master James, gentlemen." Ragged cap in hand, his blackened knees knocking slightly, the charmer turned from one to the other of us as he awaited a prompt from Holmes.

"Well, young man, what news?"

"Mr. 'olmes, I done like you as't. An' lo and be'old, out from the Post pops a gent cartin' the biggest basket ever I clapped eyes on. I about busted my gut laughin' and watchin' this bloke staggerin' down the street. An' I followed 'im to a spot called…called…"

"Come, now," Holmes gently prodded.

"The Lion! That's it. Spent quite a time there, looked at 'ome, if you knows what I mean, sir."

"Excellent, lad. And as to his appearance?"

"Oh, that. Scruffy. An' he smelled bad."

"Indeed. Anything else, Master James, concerning his appearance?"

"Oh, he was tall an' thin as a rail. An' oh yes, he limped awful bad with his lef' leg, Mr. 'olmes."

"Excellent, young man," Holmes declared, slipping a shiny coin in Master James' upturned palm. "Now, run along, little detective."

"Blimey! shouted the boy with glee as he shot through the door. An instant later, his face peered past the jamb of the door. "An' thanks, Mr. 'olmes. Be seein' ya."

No sooner had the little urchin departed when one crisp knock rang out from the door, and Catherine de Quincey entered our sitting-room. At that point, Holmes unceremoniously disappeared into his bed-room.

"What is happening, Dr. Watson?" she implored, noting the door to Holmes' room shutting fast. "Something unspeakable attacked that boy Tommy, didn't it?"

"I cannot say. Something very odd is happening, even for London."

"And Mr. Holmes, where could he be going this time of night?"

"What makes you think—"

"—Call it 'woman's intuition,' Doctor."

I promptly busied myself stacking the fireplace with logs and kindling and lit the mass aglow. "Haven't a clue. Holmes dashes out at the strangest hours. Some of his finest work is done then."

With these words, Catherine de Quincey suddenly grasped the poker by the fireplace and whipped it violently above my head as though stricken with madness and intent on knocking out my brains.

"Stop!" I shrieked.

At that moment, the poker still poised in the air, I heard a shuffling behind me. A grimy hand, brown as a nut, clapped the young woman's wrist in a vise-like grip and ever so gently twisted it till the heavy iron rod fell to the floor with a dull thud.

Out of a pocket of darkness had staggered forward a disheveled beggar in tattered rags, a grizzled yellow-white beard upon his creased, smirking face, his dwarfed stature bespeaking a lifetime of poverty and abuse. All this now melted away in an instant, in its stead the lanky, patrician figure I knew as Mr. Sherlock Holmes.

"I do believe my reactions are improving with age, Watson," he said, bowing comically in his disguise. "What think you?"

"I…I…" Catherine de Quincey could only stammer. "Is *that* really you, Mr. Holmes, beneath those…those rags? My God, I could have killed you."

"I hardly think so," Holmes scoffed.

"Your transformation, Holmes," I declared catching my breath, "is no less than magical. That beast before us only a moment ago was small in stature, nearly crippled. And here you are now with but a smudge of makeup here and there on your face and a wisp of a false beard."

"Ah, but therein lies the heart of the histrionic arts, my friend. To shed one's own characteristics and adopt another's, not so much with putty and crepe hair as with the sheer power of the imagination. That power when exercised with absolute mastery may make a giant of a dwarf, a dwarf of a giant. I take your comments as a great compliment to my poor efforts. I'm off, then, Watson. I shall see what our derelict friend has to say of strange beasts out of the pages of the Gospel." Holmes instantly snapped back into character, shrank three inches before my astonished eyes and shuffled out the door and into the night.

"This is harder than I could ever have imagined," Catherine de Quincey mumbled, more to herself than to me as she buried her head in her hand.

"What ever can you mean?" I queried.

"Only that…I have not done you and Mr. Holmes justice, bringing more trouble than aid into your lives."

I did my best to console her and sent her off to bed, I believed, in a calmer frame of mind. Apparently I drifted off within my chair only to awake with a jolt many hours later upon Holmes' return.

"Well, Holmes," I asked with an inescapable yawn and a stretch, "what news?"

"Some," Holmes tersely replied as he pulled off the rank wig and wiped make-believe grime from his gaunt face.

"After making my way to The Lion and striking up the acquaintance of the most remarkable chaps—most of whom displayed difficulty recalling their Christian names—I clapped an eye on our singular friend. He was standing at the other end of the bar begging off other beggars in a surly manner, and not surprisingly, finding little success in this enterprise. I quickly slipped out the pub and situated myself in such a way that he could not fail to notice a bottle of spirits peeking out from my threadbare side-pocket. As he limped out into the street, peering and blinking through the blackness ahead, his eyes locked onto the glittering bottleneck filled with promise, and he anxiously called to me.

"'ey mate, you, mate, how 'bout a nip?' he implored.

"'I always say drink never tastes so good as when shared with a mate; let's get comfortable here in the alley,' said I.

"Soon we emptied the bottle and were swapping life histories. Eventually I steered our conversation to the horrible story I had 'over'eard.'

"'Can you believe grown men, responsible-like, the likes of you and me, mate, fallin' for a tale the likes of that?' said I.

"'Oh, but mate, 'tis true,' he blubbered. 'Seen it with me own eyes, I did. Great hoary beasts they was, monsters, just like the Good Book says. It's all in that book, mate. Why d'ya think I'm in this state? It's nervous agitation, mate, that's wha' it is, from reading the Good Book one too many times, don't ya see?'

"'Aw, get off it, d'ya hear? If you 'spect me to swallow a 'igh-blown story the likes of that—'

"'—I tell ya, I seen 'em. Crawlin' outa' the sewers, they was.' He tipped the empty flask upside-down and pitifully pulled at the mouth with his rubbery lips. With a hapless look, he moved his craggy face within an inch of mine, Watson, to say, 'Rats, monstrous red rats 'at 'a tear your damned arm off as look at ya! I seen 'em attack tha' li'l boy. Shake them off, he did, brave li'l tyke him. One latched to his foot an' wouldn't let go. It jumped to his leg an' there it took a bite, mate. I could 'ear the juicy slosh as its 'orrible, filthy teeth sank in. An' then a fire engine clattered by an' with the noise and the light and the smoke, it must 'ave scared the bloody beasts off. It's the Gospel truth, I swears it on me mother's grave.'

"Rats, Watson. The shape of Tommy's wound corroborates the sot's story, I fear. Somehow, God knows how, London has become infested with a species of giant, man-eating rats."

CHAPTER 15

An Unexpected Visitor

I awoke with a high-pitched shriek battering my eardrums. Pulling on my dressing-gown, I stumbled into the sitting-room only to meet Holmes exclaiming, "Watson, our noble landlady. She is in distress!" He tore down the stairs as I followed in sluggish pursuit, still rubbing sleep from my eyes. Mrs. Hudson, in a paroxysm of hysterical sobs and gasps, lay crumpled at the base of the steps with wind and rain whistling past a narrow breach in the front door.

"Mr. Holmes, Mr. Holmes, the door. In Heaven's name, the door," she wailed as Catherine de Quincey, pulling on her night-dress, joined us with hesitant, measured steps.

With a look of animated expectation in Holmes' burning eyes, he and I peeked through the crack of the door to view a sight that surely thrilled both of us with horror. Through the slanted, stinging rain appeared an ashen, corded hand seemingly frozen to the exterior doorknob. Holmes' face alighted with excitement.

We attacked the door, tugging with all our might, and then the hand's outstretched arm appeared and then the remainder of the apparition, a body set in deep rigor mortis, angled nearly forty-five degrees away from the door in the most grotesque attitude. Dripping blood painted a ragged, crimson arc across the sopping entrance as Holmes and I finally swung the frame full open.

"My Lord, my Lord," Mrs. Hudson chanted plaintively, a glassy haze misting over her eyes. She was sinking into shock, and I needed to remove her immediately to a warmer room. Returning to the dreadful sight, I found Holmes engaged in dislodging the body's frozen hand from the doorknob whilst

Catherine de Quincey, growing ever more pale, looked on. Between us two, we pried free one by one the dead fingers' ghastly grip, then dragged the ungainly corpse into the center of the hallway, whereupon I hurriedly shut the door.

I could see that a terrible attack with some devilishly sharp instrument had befallen the man. I was about to speak when Holmes sternly shushed me and fell into his familiar attitude of deepest concentration. On all fours, unmindful of the sopping carpet, the swirls of blood and rainwater, Holmes circled the body, peering here and there, sniffing hound-like at an occasional, suspicious odour only he detected and clinically pulping the wound with his long, delicate fingers which he withdrew clotted in gore.

Indifferently wiping his hands on a patch of oriental rug, he finally addressed me. "Do you see anything of special interest, Watson?"

"It is all of interest to me, Holmes, but I can make nothing of it."

"I refer to the hand, his other hand."

With a gasp, Catherine de Quincey came running forward as she said, "Yes, I see it."

It was then that I noted the body's left hand and how tightly it was clasped, veins bulging even in death, with the edge of something white barely protruding from between the little finger and the side of the palm. Catherine de Quincey's hand suddenly pulled fervidly at the something but in vain.

"If you please," chided Holmes. He and I then set to freeing the object from those stiff fingers until a crumpled wad of paper fell to the floor.

Holmes' hand was the faster, and in a flash he was hastily uncrumpling a long, thin strip of paper into view. Down the length of the paper ribbon, in haphazard fashion, characters, figures and inexplicable marks had been crudely scrawled that ran as follows:

E
O 5
A
; |

; K
) N (

A N (
L C
E M

S
< S
6
_ U |
\ T

` E \
L/-

L (upside-down)

I glanced my eyes down the strip trying in vain to force some meaning into what I beheld. The marks had been written rather large, carelessly inscribed as if in haste, with long vertical gaps approximately three inches apart between some—but not all—of the marks, which I have indicated in my facsimile with additional spacing. As I stared at the tape, the scrawls proved frustratingly puzzling to me, and even Holmes' expression belied perplexity, although a twinkle in his eye spoke volumes; Holmes, I'm sure, eyed the enigma not as a problem but as a welcome challenge to his agile mind.

"Well, Watson," said Holmes, briskly rubbing his hands in delight, "how better may a day begin, eh, my friend? We have a corpse at the entrance to our home. And an intriguing cipher to bedevil the wits out of us. Whilst we ponder over all this, let us look after our landlady and see if she may throw any light upon the matter."

The three of us moved to Mrs. Hudson, swathed in the blanket I had thrown over her convulsing body and poised by the flickering fire where she was warming herself still. She seemed composed now, save for a mournful, involuntary whimper that sporadically issued from her diminutive frame.

"Mrs. Hudson, do you feel strong enough now to share your story with us?" I asked.

"Yes, thank you, Dr. Watson, I believe so," said she over one of her deep sighs. "Oh, gentlemen, Mrs. de Quincey, what a terrible way to start the day."

CHAPTER 16

Mrs. Hudson's Account

After a pause to collect her thoughts, her eyes staring absently into the distance, Mrs. Hudson recited her narrative.

"Let me see, gentlemen. As I could not sleep, I had come down to fetch a glass of warm milk for myself when I thought I heard a weak knock at the front door, and the hour being as early as it was. I asked through the closed door who it might be rapping on the door at such an hour, but all I heard was one last tap, more faint than the rest, mind you, then a thud and a long, low moan that chilled my blood, sir. Despite my better judgment, I cracked open the door, and it was then I beheld—"

Upon these words, the revisited trauma seemingly overwhelmed Mrs. Hudson, who broke down in a flood of tears. Holmes, torn between sympathy for the landlady's debilitated state and his burning desire to gain more insight, seemed compelled to press her on. "Forgive me, Mrs. Hudson, but I must ask whilst the episode remains fresh in your mind, were you able to discern any words at all?"

Struggling to regain her composure, Mrs. Hudson lamented, "No sir, not a word. Just that one horrible soul-sickening sigh."

"Thank you, Mrs. Hudson," I said. "Now, doctor's orders. You must to bed and rest."

"Just one thing more, Mrs. Hudson," Holmes interjected. "Do you recall having seen this gentleman before?"

"I saw the body, Mr. Holmes, hanging like a side of beef from our very door, but don't expect me to have looked into his face, Mr. Holmes. No, that's asking too much."

"He was nearly face down, Holmes," I commented. "She could not have had a glimpse of his face."

"Perhaps, Watson." Holmes stroked his chin and walked round in a tight circle as though debating something of delicacy to himself. "I am sorry to have to ask this of you, Mrs. Hudson—"

"—I know, Mr. Holmes," the good landlady said resignedly. "I saw his horrid, dead hand frozen to the knocker. Now, you're wantin' me to have a look at his face."

"I assure you, Mrs. Hudson, one part of his anatomy is quite as dead as another," replied Holmes with callous inattention. "But yes, could you bring yourself to…it is to our purpose."

"Yes, I suppose so," she reluctantly agreed, offering her elbow.

Holmes and I escorted our good landlady back to where the corpse lay. With delicacy, we turned over the body to reveal its face, which pivoted limply to the side, coal-black eyes upturned and stamped with the finality of death.

"Mrs. Hudson," Holmes pressed again.

The landlady slowly turned her gaze upon the ghastly visage at Holmes' feet, then quickly shut her eyes, uttering, "No, Mr. Holmes, I never—' At that moment, she raised her brows, inhaled a lungful of air as if to gather her fortitude and bent down to within inches of the livid visage, continuing, "—of all that's holy, Mr. Holmes. I have seen this gentleman!"

"When?"

"Just yesterday."

"Yesterday?" I exclaimed.

"Yes," she replied, turning her back to the body, "I had opened the door to get the second post when I noticed this man on the other side of the street."

"How came you to notice him at all, Mrs. Hudson?" Holmes asked.

"He seemed to be staring at the number of our door, Mr. Holmes. Then he removed a square of paper from his pocket, looked to be checking something written on it against our number, as if to make sure he was at the right address and then…"

"And then?" Holmes prodded impatiently.

"And then, he made a couple of steps in this direction, stopped, waited, turned round and walked a few paces down the street, stopped, turned round again, took another step or two, stopped again and finally turned back and walked off out of sight round the bend. I ask you, Mr. Holmes, how could I have missed anything peculiar as that?"

"Indeed, Mrs. Hudson. How could anyone? You have been of inestimable help. Now, you take Dr. Watson's advice and rest for the remainder of the day," Holmes decreed, ushering her by her arm back to her room.

"I think it best," Holmes said to the young lady on returning, "that you retire as well, Mrs. de Quincey."

"I am no wilting violet, gentlemen, I assure you," she responded.

"You have suffered a terrible shock, Mrs. de Quincey," I added, "and a good rest would do you no harm."

"But—"

"—No, it is for the best," Holmes declared, cutting short the young lady's objections. "More to the point, it is what I wish."

She pursed her lips, then said in a dispirited tone of voice, "Very well. Perhaps you gentlemen know best. Anyway, I've seen enough for one day." With these words, Catherine de Quincey disappeared down the creme-coloured hall.

Holmes and I returned to the grotesque, lifeless form by our doorway. Who was he, I wondered to myself, and what was the meaning—if any—of the jumble of marks on that devilish strip of paper found clutched so desperately in his hand?

As Holmes gingerly reached within the body's garments to search, I supposed, for identifying documents, I hit upon an extraordinary idea. Instead of attempting to read the message vertically, I stretched the paper tape horizontally. But, alas, the scrawls now merely rested sideways, revealing naught. Holmes caught my action, though, from the corner of his eye and shouted triumphantly, "Ah! Watson, you are brilliant. Ever the match-stick to my wick."

Holmes bounded up the stairs to our rooms two and three steps at a time. I heard him rummaging through his extraordinary collection of research materials until his voice rang out a jubilant "Halloa!" from the stair-head. In a moment, he was literally leaping down the steps with a yellowed tome in one hand and a thick tallow in the other.

"*Scytala laconias!*" Holmes cried aloud, slapping down the dusty book before me, when it parted where he had hastily inserted a thick, leather bookmark. Alas, the text was in Latin, never a strength of mine despite my life's calling. The candle was large, approximately one and a half inches in diameter and one foot and a half high.

"It is an ancient treatise," Holmes declared, "with a description of a form of encryption I believe we see an example of here before us. According to Plutarch, or so the text claims, the Lacedemonians used this method to protect their communications from peering eyes." A devilish light lit Holmes' eyes as he asked, "Watson, would you be willing to guess to what aim I intend putting this humble article?" waving the candlestick before me.

Taking up Holmes' challenge, I took the candle in hand and first considered its girth. "I dismiss its dimensions as significant outright," I declared, with more than a dollop of pomposity in my manner on hindsight. "Merely a quality of the first candle you came across, Holmes." I next studied its height and colour with an air of professional intensity. "Rather than any physical characteristic," I continued, "the key lies in the candle's function. I should say, Holmes," feeling a bit self-congratulatory with the manner in which I had come to my conclusion, "that this candle—lit—reveals characters somehow hidden within the paper strip, itself." With these words, I raised the tape before the glow of the fireplace and peered into its very fibres in quest of the slightest affirmation of my theory. "Or…that the heat of its flame reveals marks written with invisible ink of some remarkable composition to complete the message."

Holmes released a deep mournful sigh, uttering, "Watson, Watson, I am sorry to say that I cannot congratulate you. You have grievously erred in a way too common to many, both in decisions mediocre and of the utmost gravity. Sadly, you dismissed your first inclination, which happened to be the correct one, as is often the case. The candle's girth is, in fact, a key element. A diameter either too small in the slightest or too large by a hair would not deliver satisfactory results."

Despite his animadversion of my abilities, Holmes had managed to pique my curiosity to a fever pitch. "How then, Holmes, can you possibly make sense of these scrawls with a simple candle?" I testily challenged.

The shadow of a grin playing upon his thin lips, Holmes directed me to hold the candle sideways by either end. Then he performed a remarkable act. He pressed the tape into the soft wax of the tallow at one end and began wrapping the strip diagonally round the thick body of the candle, finally affixing the remainder of the strip into the other end of the candle with his thumbnail. Miraculously, the coarse characters and unidentifiable marks now fell in place into two lines that read as follows:

A ;KAN(EM< S_UI-E\ L (upside-down)
EO5; |)N(LCS 6\TL/-

We stared at the lines as if waiting for them to speak back, bark or do *something*.

"Do you," I inquired of Holmes, "make anything of this?"

"In a word, no. Watson," Holmes admitted, "I have failed." He exhaled a deep sigh and turned the candle with its cryptic message round in his hands. "I'm sorry, dear friend, I thought I had it."

"Perhaps you revealed some second conundrum to be unraveled, Holmes."

"I think not, Watson," he said. "Our dead friend does not strike me as having possessed the faculties for being that clever. This method is old and, though little known in most parts of the world, would eventually have touched the life of a man such as he, I think, in one of his exotic travels. He did not invent the method on his own and certainly did not embellish upon it."

One end of the tape suddenly broke free of the wax and its length curled and bounced like a toy spring. Suddenly, Holmes' eyes lit up!

"Do you see it, Watson?" he cried. "Of course, that's the diabolical point about this method. If you don't have the right size dowel or candle or other cylindrical object to work with, then the message comes out all scrambled."

"Ah, I'll run up and find another candle—"

"—No, Watson, don't bother," he exclaimed. "In this case, the candle is the right size. One other step must be performed correctly," Holmes continued, detaching the tape from the tallow and running it through his slender fingers. "One must begin wrapping it in the correct direction, as well."

A broad smile of triumph upon his face, Holmes rewrapped the tape around the candle and the message in two lines now clearly revealed itself, which read as follows:

TELUK SEMANGKA
LAT 6 S LONG 105 E

"A location on the globe. Congratulations, man!" I exclaimed, heartily slapping his back.

"So we have our message, Watson," Holmes said, his eyes gleaming. In the vicinity of the Malay Archipelago, I should guess."

We scrambled upstairs to the great globe of Mother Earth that Holmes kept secure in a corner of our sitting-room. Spinning the orb round frantically to and fro, we located where the latitude and longitude coordinates crossed, a point by the long, jagged scar that was the island of Sumatra.

CHAPTER 17

An Identity Revealed

Light was just breaking when I left Mr. Sherlock Holmes at his globe and cracked open the door of 221 B, Baker Street. A faint mist swirled at my feet, and the brisk air bit at the exposed flesh of my face and hands whilst I reviewed the extraordinary events of this morning in my mind: Mrs. Hudson's frightful screams, the lifeless form at my doorstep, its reach for aid frozen in a macabre *tableau,* an encrypted note seemingly mandating beyond the grave that Holmes and I blindly follow a treacherous course into the unknown.

Hailing one of the lads who habitually loiter nearby in hope of an occasional odd chore, I handed the street arab a shilling, instructing him to deliver my note with haste to the nearest police station with the promise of a shilling more should he return with the constables within fifteen minutes.

Not ten minutes passed before the young lad gleefully reappeared—his hand out for the second coin—delivering a police inspector, detective and constable to the door. I escorted in the representatives of the law, then Holmes explained what had occurred, taking care to disclose the barest of details. Holmes' reputation shielded him and me from the slightest suspicion in the matter, and after an insignificant inquiry or two from the police detective the stalwart representatives of the law departed. By the end of the hour, four constables came lugging a stretcher and unceremoniously removed the body.

I looked in on our landlady and was relieved to find her sleeping peacefully, after which Holmes and I withdrew upstairs to the privacy of our sitting-room.

"Holmes," I implored, lighting a cigarette and drawing the smoke in deeply, "what then do you make of our visitor?"

"On first glance, Watson, I knew the man to have been a sailor," Holmes expounded. He filled his long clay pipe with strong shag tobacco and held a lit match-stick to its bowl. A blue-grey cloud billowed from Holmes' location upon the velvet chair, smoky arabesques swirling and hugging the folds of his dressing-gown with his every move. "The documents I found on his person," he continued as he handed me a thin packet of worn papers wadded together with an India-rubber band, "merely corroborated the tell-tale callosities on his hands, the state of his nails, the leathery aspect of his flesh, as a man of the sea, but, alas, the papers reveal little else. We must put great stock in one fact, Watson." Holmes paused dramatically to relight his pipe before continuing his thought. "This man sacrificed his life to deliver the message to us."

"One other fact is singular, Holmes," I added. "The attack was brutal. The instrument penetrated the entire body from back to front, piercing his heart on its unhappy journey, thus the enormous loss of blood. Only a powerful thrust could have inflicted such terrible damage. But can you not tell me more as to his identity?"

"His boots are of some interest, Watson. They are clotted with a type of mud with which I am not familiar, and bits of small blades of vegetation and petals within the caked earth are nowhere to be found to my knowledge upon this continent. My guess? That they are from the Sumatran region to which the message alludes and that this unfortunate guest of ours had recently returned from just such a journey.

"Despite his harsh occupation and the brutish appearance of the man, he wore a simple cross, Watson, about his neck, and the single tattoo upon his person is of Mary. We have even learnt from Mrs. Hudson that he was here only the day before, standing mere paces from our lodgings, some internal battle underway between his better half and that side of him that had made harder choices in life. I believe him to have been a decent, devout man. I can only surmise that after a long series of transgressions, his conscience eventually touched some inmost core of his being."

"And in an ill-fated act of redemption, Holmes, he returned with a secret message, only to meet his death."

"Just so, and now the puzzle is near completion, Watson. Recall each singular, seemingly disconnected incident we have experienced together over the last several weeks: A typewriting machine mysteriously stolen from a destitute, infirm cowhand and a calculating device stolen from one Lucy Gates: Shadowy agents following behind with the slightest of steps: Warnings of doom from beyond from the lips of a sensitive: The attempted theft of documents belonging to an obscure monk living a quiet, secluded life: Missing manuscripts containing Charles Darwin's inmost speculations on the essence of man and of Nature and threats against him and his family: Horrid attacks on Tommy, on a little girl named Laura and on others by some vicious, hitherto unknown species of beast: And now a murdered messenger at our very doorstep beckoning us to a forsaken edge of the world. All these occurrences have now settled in my imagination into one cohesive whole, and I must tell you, Watson, that the vision is horrific. Unthinkable scientific experiments have been taking place by the power of some unimaginable engine and guided by the force of a dark, malevolent intellect as yet uncertain to us.

"But I am convinced that we are now armed with the latitude and longitude of its vile source, a cesspool of evil, whose fetid waters radiate in every direction to poison all that they touch. The time has come to act, my friend, before the world is lost to us. To Sumatra, Watson, Sumatra!"

CHAPTER 18

Sumatra Calls

It was starkly evident to Holmes and to me that Fate had left us little recourse. We were now set upon a long and treacherous journey: Travelling to a mystery-laden location in the steaming jungles of the Sumatra region and taking whatever measures we deemed necessary to deny a faceless opponent further opportunity to perpetuate his evil machinations.

Contrasting with the epic course upon which Holmes and I had steered ourselves, the grim reality of the financial burden we were about to incur set in. To aid in defraying expenses, Holmes and I withdrew what savings we had whilst Holmes conferred with his brother, Mycroft, to secure a speedy sale of his treasured snuff box, the jewel-encrusted momento given him by a grateful member of one of the royal families of Europe.

Although I had not yet met Mycroft, I came to understand that Holmes often consulted with his brother in pursuing the occasional, odd snippet of knowledge, particularly when his other wellspring of the bizarre, one Langdale Pike, was occupied elsewhere. Should the location of the popular opium establishment of the day be required or the identity of the currently blackmailed member of royal society be advantageous, Mycroft was the man to whom Holmes turned as much as when the great detective needed at his fingertips the whereabouts of a certain forger or of a counterfeiter.

It was my understanding that, though Mycroft had no personal enthusiasm in direct participation, he satisfied a nearly morbid curiosity about the darker activities of the City by following and recording the histories of those who would indulge in or were caught up in London's seamier side. In like fashion,

Mycroft was expert in Holmes' eyes in recollecting all manner of details concerning the obscure, the obtuse and even the obscene or—as in Holmes' present situation—an avenue of quick sale for an article of delicate or suspect lineage.

Our assets pooled, given such slight notice I could secure but one vessel that even remotely met our pressing needs, a schooner named the *Alice Fair* bound for Singapore and set to sail from Liverpool in little more time than Holmes and I should arrive at the bustling port via train. By wire and with the aid of a hefty monetary inducement, the master of the schooner, one Captain A. R. Paulsen, reluctantly agreed to delay his departure till our arrival and to keep the nature of our contract in confidence from his crew as best he could.

The morning of our departure, Holmes left earlier than I to settle some last minute accounts, with the intention of meeting me at the station. As the time approached to collect my belongings, I found the landlady in the pantry and took her aside, saying, "Mrs. Hudson, remember that Mr. Holmes and I shall be away for some time. Just how long I cannot say."

"I pray your trip will not be too dangerous for you and Mr. Holmes," she said maternally.

"No, not at all," I falsely assured her. "Now, Mrs. Hudson, do you recall a young lady who came visiting recently?"

"A Miss Gates?"

"Excellent, Mrs. Hudson, you've quite a memory. Should she…come calling, would you be so kind as to inform her that I shall be away for some time, but that I shall want to see her as soon as I return?"

"Of course, Doctor."

"And this, most important of all, please ask for some means of contacting her."

"You mean—"

"—Yes, Miss Gates has gone missing."

"My word! The things that do happen here."

"Quite. Now, I want a word with Catherine de Quincey before I leave. Do you know if she is in her room?"

"She is not," Mrs. Hudson said sharply. "Frankly, we got in a bit of a fray, Dr. Watson, and she stomped out a few moments ago like a petulant child."

"You don't say?" I queried rhetorically. "Pray tell me precisely what occurred."

"She said that she knew something odd was afoot and asked about Mr. Holmes and if I knew what it was that was going on. I told her I did not, that it was no more any of her business than mine and that if I did know more, I'd not share it with her in the first place. It was then she accused me of keeping the truth from her and implored me to share whatever I knew with her, claiming that she had become very concerned for Mr. Holmes' safety. When I made it clear I had nothing more to say, she became angry and perturbed, which is when she tore out the door in a fit."

"You did well," I said to the loyal landlady, her cheeks slightly flushed with the passion of her account.

As curious as Catherine de Quincey's behavior struck me at the time, the incident quickly exited my mind with the press of final preparations for the journey. I arrived at Euston Station in time to meet my companion and to begin our dramatic excursion with the Liverpool express.

By the time Holmes and I alighted at the Liverpool dock at forenoon in our hired trap, the captain had busied his crew with the minutiae of preparing the vessel for her long voyage ahead. He had a seaman swung precariously out over the prow stalwartly chipping away fist-sized flakes of rust from the anchor with a hefty iron pick whilst another slapped paint upon the raw metal from the sagging bristles of a well-worn brush. A small army of seamen were occupied at whittling new belaying pins to replace the ones worn down by the coarse ropes' endless sawing back and forth. Still others of the hapless crew fastidiously swabbed the deck of the previous voyage's salt spray and debris.

Captain Paulsen stood prominently at the helm surveying all, directing an unending stream of commands and reprimands at his crew. The general word was that he had an extraordinary career spanning greater than thirty years in the hard and fiercely competitive world of the commercial packet-ship business and had seen everything there was to be seen at sea. His was a square-jawed countenance if ever I saw one, with stern, ice-blue eyes that peered through tight slits as he oversaw his men. A large black Labrador lashed by a sturdy strap of brown leather sat attentively by his side, its head swinging to and fro keenly following the seeming chaos of activity all about with an occasional glance up for a wink of approval from his master.

"Captain Paulsen," I exclaimed as we scrambled up the boarding plank, "it is I, Dr. Watson, and my companion, Mr. Sherlock Holmes."

"You took your time well enough, gentlemen," he barked, looking us up and down, "but by God, the wind's about right. We'll cast her off. Come aboard!"

The captain bellowed a stream of commands to his men to prepare to set sail. The final crates were quickly hoisted into the cargo hold, and the last of the steerage passengers mulling about the forecastle were led down the steps to the 'tween deck. When all was secure, an officer conveyed the ship's readiness to the captain.

Captain Paulsen was of the old school of seamanship who disdained the practice of using a tug in escaping the berth. He moved to the starboard side of the quarter-deck and bellowed into a speaking trumpet for the topsails and jibs to be hoisted and the spankers loosened. When the sails caught wind, he kept a keen watch on the lines, for this was an especially dangerous and critical step in the launch. The cables strained audibly with an ominous pinging when he ordered them cast off and the schooner began backing out of the dock. The *Alice Fair's* rigging was alive with seamen now, shifting her jibs and topsails to turn her stern upstream into the Mersey River and out to sea.

Holmes and I were finally off. Once well out to sea, Captain Paulsen called us into the privacy of his cabin, taking the precaution of bolting the cabin door. He wore a taut expression on his face as he gestured for us to be seated.

"Well, gentlemen," said he, "with a bit of luck, according to my charts, we should make the Sumatran coastline, give or take, within 25 days. But only by travelling night and day in the manner of packet-ships. That's going to put a severe strain on both ship and crew—"

The cabin door rattled. I could see two men through the cabin window exchanging distressed glances as one of them tried the door again, then they grudgingly parted.

"—Anything could happen," continued the captain.

"Then there's the Sumatra region, itself. It's dangerous, a volcanic hell, and our destination more dangerous still with the island's low-lying topography. Then there's the island's U-shaped coastline, directly facing active volcanoes in the region.

"Have you any idea what damage a giant wave can do? Saw one myself once when I was young, and I'll tell you now, the sight's seared in my soul forever.

"Believe me, it's all an invitation to disaster. I only hope you know what you're doin', gentlemen," Captain Paulsen said, wiping sweat from his brow. "And that it's worth the gamble."

"I assure you, Captain," replied Holmes, "it's worth the gamble."

"God bless us all, then," Captain Paulsen gravely declared.

Holmes and I left him alone in his cabin, shaken with his troubling disclosures but determined more than ever to persevere.

Neither Holmes nor I was accustomed to journeying for so long by ship, although Holmes once mentioned that he had travelled to America in his youth. As for me, following my convalescence in Peshawar, I last sailed on the troopship *Orontes* back to England. The unpredictable sea and weather and the limited comfort afforded by the *Alice Fair's* cabin little helped the days pass by. Truth to tell, personal comfort was the last thought on our minds, so focused upon the mission were we both.

On the third and fourth day, several black squalls threatened the *Alice Fair*, huge, swelling waves pitching our vessel to and fro as though a toy whilst driving sheets of rain blurred beyond recognition any view past the bulwarks of the ship. Only by Captain Paulsen's decisive handling of the *Alice Fair* did we survive the violence of those terrible gails. The immediacy of near disaster recalled to mind a cherished phrase by Horace I had learnt by rote as a child: *"Surely oak and three-fold brass surrounded his heart who first trusted a frail vessel to a merciless ocean."* In youthful ignorance, these words had often thrilled me with many a romantic notion, but now they only engulfed me with dread, the hard reality of present and foreshadowed dangers.

The next several days, however, proved relatively uneventful, though I often observed heavy clouds sweeping upon the horizon and threatening more squalls. Fortuitously, they failed to materialize near us. Save for the excitement of the day we passed through the newly constructed Suez Canal with her massive locks, boredom weighed heavily upon me.

At such times, I would try to alleviate the monotony by carefully tending to the Eley's No. 2, my trusty service-revolver that I had tossed in my portmanteau at Holmes' request along with explosives and wiring devices he deemed necessary for our mission. I would also scribble copious notes about the evolving case to refine upon our return and would discourse with Holmes as to what our strategy might be on landing.

In contrast to a succession of days sporting little drama, I grew increasingly aware of dark clouds growing not in the sky but amongst several of the crew, a vague discontent whose cause I failed to discern from the fragments of conversation I overheard during feigned constitutionals on deck.

One morning, the helmsman ignored a "steer steady" order from Captain Paulsen who issued it again, salted with expletives and booming finally, "You'll hear my orders but once, Mister, or you'll do your listening in irons from the brig."

"Get a whiff of that, Cap'n, will ye?" the recalcitrant sailor snapped back. Suddenly a strong sulfuric odour assaulted my sense of smell. "If you think I don't know what—"

"Smell or no smell," Captain Paulsen cut in with his booming voice, "I give the orders here, and you'll obey them, or you'll find yourself food for the sharks below, do you hear, man?"

The helmsman acceded to the captain's command, his mouth spraying silent profanities into the air whilst reluctantly executing the order. The pungent odour of sulfur stung my nostrils as I heard a grumbling rise from the sailors on deck sluggishly going about their duties.

As the helmsman passed, I caught him by the arm and asked, "That odour. You know what it is?"

"Damn volcano," he hissed through his yellow teeth. "If only you knew—"

The sound of Captain Paulsen clearing his throat was all the helmsman needed to break away and continue his duties. The acrid malodour lingered in the air, and I my ears detected what sounded like the rumbling of distant thunder though the sky was bright and clear.

Next evening a meal with Holmes was interrupted by sharp raps on our cabin door. The second mate, pale and drawn, entered and when he did so, our ears were assailed by the sound of impassioned discord coming from somewhere on deck.

The officer entreated, "Gentlemen, you had best come up to the quarter-deck. The captain veered off course to meet his pact with you, and suddenly there's some serious mischief brewing among the hands. The captain thought he might need your assistance in putting aright the situation."

When we reached Captain Paulsen, he was standing staunchly before the setting sun, a cocked pistol in each hand and pointed in the direction of the rowdy group of malcontents not three paces before him shaking their fists and raised, threatening pinions in his face.

"We put up with secrets enough, Cap'n," grumbled an acid-faced seaman acting as spokesman. "We put it to a vote just now, you see, and we've a right to know why you've gone and changed course on us. There's our marker," the brown hand pointing to a gently sloping volcanic formation rising starboard in the distance, a small, white plume hovering at the tip of its blunt cone, "and we listing to the left instead of following her guide into Selat Sunda and onto Singapore. What say you to that, Cap'n?"

"You'll drive this ship to hell and back if I order it so," blasted Captain Paulsen defiantly, the cocked pistols swaying ever so slightly in his hands from man to man. Their venomous eyes glared back upon the captain who uttered more threats with his scowling, deep-set brows than ever their tongues could issue.

"We signs up to sail with you one place and here you shanghais the lot of us to somewheres else. The word's out that we're headed for a bit of hell on earth in Teluk Semangka!"

"I heard it whispered," said another, a purple scar running down the length of his ruddy face, "it be an area of Sumatra that's damned, cursed. And cursed are all foolhardy enough to venture there, Cap'n, is what they say. Strange things doing there. Stranger yet the beasts sighted there. And many who step on its shores never returning dead or alive. Is this the forsaken place you're forcing us to, Cap'n, again' our wills?"

"By God, you've sailed with me many a year, Smithers, and you, O'Brien, and you, Prestwick!" bellowed Captain Paulsen. "All of you, but especially you men whose names I just called, know that the safety of the ship and my crew stands above all else. But be that as it may, I'm captain here and you sail where I say you sail, *damn you all!*"

With these words, one of the men jumped forward, yelling, "Slit the bloody blackguard's throat," and drawing his sheath-knife. Holmes leapt panther-like before the sailor, striking a straight left against the ruffian and hurtling him on his back with some little violence before Captain Paulsen's feet. The great Labrador vaulted upon the sailor's chest, pinning him down along with bared fangs and menacing growls.

"Listen to me, men!" Holmes shouted, "your captain has changed course to serve my purposes but only to drop me and my companion off at a certain location. Yes, our destination is in the Semangka bay, an insignificant piece of land, hardly worth calling an island, off an unexplored region of the main Island of Sumatra. But no one asks anything of you save a moment's patience as we disembark. From there you shall continue on to your original destination, the captain and I pledge you that."

"We hain't bound to await your return, then," asked Smithers, clearing his parched throat, "or to aid in whatever dark business is yours there?"

The captain jumped in, saying, "No, men. Arrangements have been made for another ship heading back to Liverpool to pick up Mr. Holmes and his companion three days hence. No one asks anything of you but to obey your orders as you always have. If I'd have known the destination these gentlemen were bound for had such a terrible reputation or would have such an ill effect on your imaginations, well, I might have shared my secret with you. Or not taken on the job in the first place. If you're looking for an apology, that's the closest you'll get from me, damn you all to Hades!"

Two officers stepped up, one with clinking shackles in hand, and bent to the sailor pinned by the magnificent Labrador when the captain's voice boomed out, "No gentlemen, this one's a good lad. He's a hot-head, for sure. The heat of the moment got to his better sense, that's all. Off, Blackstone."

Upon command, the great Labrador obediently lifted its massive frame off the mutinous sailor and scrambled back to its place by the side of its master. The crewman hopped up brandishing an awkward grin upon his bruised face, and backed away with many a respectful bow of his head as the rest of the crew quietly dispersed, returning to their respective duties.

"That was a close one," muttered the second mate to himself.

"Return to your posts," Captain Paulsen gruffly commanded, addressing his officers and sliding the now uncocked pistols back under his belt. "Well, you've caused your share of trouble for one day, gentlemen," he declared, scowling at Holmes and me beneath his bushy, salt-and-pepper brows and sharply turning away to the wheel.

To tell the truth, Holmes and I breathed a strong sigh of relief when we returned to our cabin. "That *was* very close," Holmes admitted. "If only these men knew how near they came to disrupting a mission of the utmost consequence."

Holmes withdrew into himself for the remainder of the hour, sending unending curls of smoke into the air from his meditative pipe whilst my blood stirred with the knowledge that we were now rapidly approaching our mystery-laden destination. From that moment, my trusty Eley's No. 2 hugged my side, tucked snugly in readiness under my belt.

CHAPTER 19

The Gates of Hell

Finally, the island came into view. The second mate led us to Captain Paulsen, peering into a night as black as creosote save for flashes of dim silver tracings of palm frond when the moon would momentarily break through a thick, building cloud-bank. We could hear the lapping of waves upon the shore only a couple of hundred yards away and the musical rustling of tropical leaves.

"Well, gentlemen," said the captain, "this is where you take your leave. We'll lower you two in a boat and wish God speed. The steamer *Matilda Briggs* is expected to pass by in three days' time and I trust she finds you ship-shape.

"Her crew'll not be any happier than mine to pass through these waters, but a deal's a deal. Just know she'll not wait a second longer than need be, so drill your signals well and keep to the shore. If there's nothing else—"

Suddenly a faint sound—as of a cork popping from a bottle of champagne—met our ears. Our eyes were drawn to a dim orange glow flickering in the distance, delineating prickly silhouettes of palm trees waving in the dark beyond. The glow increased until our eyes clearly beheld lapping tongues of flame and shafts of sparks like Roman candles shooting into the air.

Throwing his head back in a sudden, raucous laugh of resignation, Holmes cried out, "Well, Watson, I think our friend has beaten us at our game." Then, more seriously, "this may be *it*, old friend!"

"Do you mean—"

I never completed my sentence. An ear-shattering explosion ripped the schooner in twain, splinters of wood and iron flying in all directions like a swarm of fierce wasps whilst white-hot flames shot out from every gaping cavity of the *Alice Fair's* broken hull. All too quickly, the sea rose up around me, and I lost sight of Holmes.

Paddling past bodies bobbing face-down and broken bits of spars, burning fragments of sail falling everywhere about me, I felt my feet suddenly touch sand, and in a moment I was pushing myself by the palms of my hands with all my strength up a cove just above the lapping waters. Like the waves, the darkness lapped in and out around me. I peered back into the great black span of silhouette that was the sea and called out Holmes' name repeatedly.

After an eternity—or so it seemed—a black form rose up from the water's edge and my hand moved instinctively to the revolver; it was lost to the sea. My heart leapt when I heard a voice answer breathlessly back, "It is I, Watson," the flickering light from innumerable fires delineating Holmes' hawk-like face. We shamelessly embraced, so happy were we to find either alive.

Then Holmes declared, "Look there!" pointing in the direction of a glow under the waves. As I looked in astonishment, I discerned that the glow was a row of broad points of light like ports spilling forth yellow illumination from a ship-sized craft just underneath the waves.

"In the name of all that is holy, Holmes, tell me what my eyes behold!" I exclaimed, clapping my head in my hands.

"Yes, I've read of this, Watson. Forgive me for taking my leave so soon after our happy reunion," said Holmes, "but I must take a closer look, my friend." He dove back into the black water as my heart leapt to my throat.

The moonlight broke through, and I saw Holmes' thrashing arms and legs advancing him straight in the direction of the ghostly craft suspended under the lapping waters. I could see his form pass before one of the glowing ports, then disappear completely.

Time passed like hours, but it was only a moment before Holmes' head bobbed back into view a few yards away. I leapt to my feet and waded in quickly to aid him back to shore. He was gasping for air, but a grin of triumph, nevertheless, shone upon his face.

"What in the world have you to say?" I exclaimed with astonishment.

"Amazing! It is an underwater craft of some advanced design, Watson, all metallic skin and bolts, humming with the heart of some great, mysterious engine. The incomparable Leonardo envisioned such a mechanism hundreds of years ago, and I have seen secret documents purporting that such devices were used during the war between the states in America and even before, during their revolution."

"Oh, by the way," added Holmes, displaying his left hand before me.

In my joy at finding Holmes standing before me, I failed to notice he had been shielding his left hand behind his back. Now I found myself staring at my beloved Eley's, saltwater streaming from its barrel.

"I spotted something familiar, Watson, and thought you'd enjoy its return to its rightful owner."

"Bless you, Holmes!" I exclaimed.

He paused to take some well-deserved deep breaths, then grasped me intensely by my wet lapels.

"Watson, Watson, I saw him!" he said fiercely. "I swam straight to one of the ports behind which his huge visage suddenly appeared, and we instantly locked eyes. I knew it was he, he knew I was Sherlock Holmes. He pierced me with dead, black pupils, the lifeless eyes of a shark, Watson. And laughing all the while, shaking a great, wild mane of silvery hair. Laughing until a surge of bubbles rose violently from beneath the craft and the strange vessel darted away with incredible speed, nearly knocking me unconscious with the violence of its wake. I watched the glowing ports rapidly shrink, then disappear.

"The nameless villain has destroyed his own facilities, murdered a shipful of men, women and children, who knows how many. It is quite on the cards that he is now heading back to his other base somewhere in London under the power of that marvelous machine, and he has left us here for dead."

Holmes stared ahead into the blackness beyond, a stern, unwavering look of determination upon his face. "Yes, I can see him still, laughing," Holmes said through his teeth, "laughing at us all this very moment.

"We shall see who laughs last."

With a late-dawning sense of obligation, Holmes and I set to searching for any souls who might have survived the terrible ambush. Behind a clump of mangroves some hundred paces down the coastline, we discovered a ragged group of survivors, among them the bo'sun and first mate of the *Alice Fair* and what remained of three families from steerage class.

I ministered to the injured, doing what I could without my medical satchel; most of their injuries were serious but not life-threatening. The best in Holmes' character came shining through as he moved from one to the other of the injured and stunned, offering little kindnesses and pats on the head to the children, and reminding all that a schooner would be arriving within three days to take them to safety.

After assisting them to build a small fire around which they all gravitated and huddled, Holmes and I moved on when a woman hugging her two children suddenly gasped. Frightened eyes stared up at me as she cried, "Somethin' moved behind that there bush, somethin' large, with red eyes."

"Come, now," I said, "I think you heard nothing more than the rustling of leaves."

"It weren't no plant, sir," she replied.

"At any rate," Holmes offered, "the fire shall stay any beasts foraging through the jungle. Keep it burning and you shall have nothing to fear."

We moved on, discovering a battered sailor at the far edge of the shoal who had suffered numerous injuries including a broken left arm and right thigh and third-degree burns over much of his body. Sad to say, I could do little for the young man and by morning, he had mercifully passed away. By the time we laid him in a quick, shallow grave, Holmes and I could walk or talk no longer, and we scrambled up to a small, dry patch of vegetation to fall into a deep, welcoming sleep.

And so Holmes and I found ourselves on an unexplored bit of tropical reef awaiting the passage of the *Matilda Briggs* two days thence. Perhaps, I hoped, a rescue ship would swing by even earlier once the *Alice Fair* failed to be spotted en route or once her flotsam and jetsam were noted by some vigilant observer.

On awakening, I found Holmes, myself and our surroundings dusted with a light-grey, talc-like ash, and the sky had taken on a dense, copperish colour. My ears pricked, too, at a distant, ominous rumbling. I recalled the peak and its plume of smoke one of the sailors had pointed to as we neared the island and the warnings earlier on from Captain Paulsen. My thoughts carried me away to my youth and, with a shudder, to my readings of the terrible events that occurred in ancient Pompeii. I could not help but wonder if this island, with all its threats, was where I would meet my end without the chance of seeing my Lucy one more time, of hearing her musical voice or of holding her ivory hand in mine.

Hunger, however, made its inevitable appearance, and I managed however clumsily to catch crab for breakfast for Holmes and myself. Then we decided to explore the area of the fire still sending up corkscrews of smoke into the air. We scrambled through tall cane, sharp-spurred thickets that cut at our heels and skirted around blistered pools of gurgling mud belching malodorous fumes. At one point, we sank knee-deep into green, sponge-like mosses infested with buzzing, stinging mosquitoes and with slithering vipers. By the shape of the head, I knew they were venomous and cautioned Holmes more than once on a serpent's approach.

As we trudged forward, the mud and slime beneath our feet firmed up. The hour grew hot and full of the drone of gnat-like insects, the muscles in my thighs burning now with every step. Suddenly the earth liquefied, undulating in powerful waves that flung Holmes and me to the ground. The shaking continued spasmodically as grey ash from the sky lightly dusted us again.

Holmes flicked ash from his lids as he said, "A fine place to visit, eh, Watson? Fires, explosions and, now, volcanic ash spewing from somewhere uncomfortably nearby."

In a moment, the trembling subsided, and we continued on as a light rain of the grey cinders persisted. We passed more steaming geysers and patches of swamp, in the distance thickets of dark-green bushes, creepers and yellow cane. Finally—hours later, it seemed—the strange mist of grey soot subsided.

Now my nostrils filled with the acrid smell of smoking vegetation, and I knew that we were very near our destination. Another few, painful paces brought us before the charred skeleton of a long architectural structure, crackling with the tongues of myriad small flames, no remnant of Nature's violence but the handiwork of a villain whose demise Holmes and I had sworn to effect.

The smoking vestige of the structure's low, rectangular form reminded me of greenhouses I had visited along the English countryside, except that they had been filled with life and beauty; the structure before us spoke only of death, horror and decay.

I shook my head dejectedly, muttering, "All is lost, Holmes. What can one make of this?"

"If only you made the effort to see rather than merely to look, Watson. Then you would note tell-tale broken bits of glass at your feet. They once formed retorts, balloon flasks, test-tubes and other equipment common to scientific pursuit. This was a laboratory of some type, surely. A child of five could have come to that conclusion, Watson," Holmes disdainfully declared.

He suddenly shut his eyes and pressed his palms to his temples. "Forgive me, Watson, forgive me. Nothing disturbs me more than wanton destruction. I was overwhelmed for the moment. Think, Holmes…think…reason."

He kept muttering this phrase to himself as we toured the blackened shell and its contents, all the while kicking mounds of debris aside with our feet. One more thrust of my foot suddenly sent a tangle of oddly-shaped skeletal remains clattering into view. Holmes' brows arched with interest as he whipped round and stooped before the macabre mass.

"What say you, Watson," Holmes asked with a thrill in his voice, "are these…human?"

"Yes. And no, Holmes," I replied, studying the misshapen remains before me. "I see bits and pieces of human-like structures, the remnants of three poor souls, I believe, but the twisted forms…"

"Yes, they are singularly repulsive. Might these deformations in any way have been caused by a virulent form of arthritis?"

"I think not, Holmes. I have never seen so gross an effect from the disease. In fact, I can think of nothing that may have caused such terrible distortions save some monstrous defect at birth."

"These poor remains must point to only one conclusion, Watson: The result of experimentation on a nightmarish scale. Let us see what else we may find," Holmes declared.

We continued pacing the blackened hull of the structure until I heard Holmes exclaim, "Halloa!" reaching downward into the ash and lifting a heavy trap door by a massive iron knocker. Peering in we observed with horror pile upon pile of bone, human bone, displaying minute variations of the same terrible deformations we had discovered moments ago.

"My God, Holmes, what sort of madman are we dealing with?" I cried.

"I vow that I shall answer that question very soon in returning home, Watson."

"What was that?" I suddenly exclaimed upon hearing a startling noise, like air violently expelled from the nostrils of a great beast. Holmes started, too, and picked up a large brick of volcanic rock to fend off…what? Something at the extremity of the building's blackened frame was moving, kicking up knots of dust that made any clear impression of it all the more difficult for us. Holmes took aim and hurled the sharp-edged rock into the rising yellow cloud, something squealed loudly and tromped off, parting shoots of bamboo in its path. As the dust cleared we walked up to the spot where Holmes had aimed the projectile. It lay in a pool of bright red blood, matted with coarse red hairs which Holmes bent to for closer inspection. The slender, nervous fingers of his right hand lifted one of the hairs close to his keen eyes.

"I think I have said this to you before," stated Holmes solemnly. "It is the hair of a rat, Watson. A very large red rat."

With sharp eye and ear, Holmes and I began the short but trying journey back to the general area of shoal on which we had earlier beached. We found the other souls in various states of languor, limp bodies slumped here and there in surrender to the oppressive, tropical heat, beating back swarms of mosquitoes with frenetic waving of the hands, children wailing in discomfort.

Holmes implored all to remain close to shore for the remaining day, God willing, emphasizing the abundance of edible fruit and crab, and reminding all of the unknown facing anyone straying into the jungle. He especially stressed keeping an eye out for what he named "wild boar," and the merit of the old dictum of strength in numbers.

We passed the final hours as best we could. The second mate, a chap named Stamford, discovered a pad of note-paper that had dried in the sun in that distinctively crinkled manner that dried paper pulp adopts, and with the charcoal of burnt twigs drew a pack of cards upon the slips of paper with which he induced us to play various games of chance, using shells we collected as our tokens. A couple of other survivors rigged up a crude tent-like structure out of palm fronds and bamboo under which they perched, staring hopefully out upon the sea in search of an early rescue.

Holmes himself was in a constant state of agitation, strutting to and fro on the fine sand, who knows what thoughts racing with lightning speed through his agile mind. Alas, he could do little else as he—like the rest—bode his time.

No unfamiliar rescue ship ever passed by. But the steamer, the *Matilda Briggs*, finally appeared on the horizon, not on the third but on the fourth day. Everyone hurriedly gathered kindling into a grand pile, and someone got the woody tangle blazing. We collectively puffed and fanned the fire till a great, black cloud arose. We sent the smoky signal into the air repeatedly until we could see the longboats being rowed ashore.

Suddenly, a distant booming met our ears whilst the sky took on the colour of lead. The ground began violently shaking, and a hellish rain of choking ash fell to the accompaniment of fiery showers of orange sparks. With the assault, a chorus of screams and wails rose up from the assemblage.

One man by the shoreline caught the fury of blazing pumice stone and dove into the rising waters to the hiss of steam. A woman to my immediate left burst into flame from the molten debris. Before I had my chance, Holmes leapt to her aid, flinging great handfuls of sand upon her torched flesh and clothing. I joined in Holmes' efforts and waved everyone on to take shelter where they may.

The sea, too, turned fierce, violently pelting the mother ship and her longboats halfway to shore with wave upon merciless wave. One longboat capsized, spilling its crew into the swelling tides. Sea salts though they may have been, many found themselves sucked under by the pull of ferocious riptides. Others grappled to cling to the upended hull.

As swiftly as the quakes and vicious tides began, they subsided, though a lesser downpour of stifling ash continued along with occasional flurries of glowing embers. The last round of fierce waves mercifully beached the upturned longboat and several sailors scrambled to flip over her hull. As her battered sister boats arrived, Holmes and I goaded and shoved stunned survivors into hastily boarding the rocking vessels. Powerful arms cut the longboats through inches of ash that had settled on the sea during the volcanic storm.

Finally, Holmes and I watched as the ragged party—spectre-like in their coats of grey ash—shuffled aboard the *Matilda Briggs*, weak smiles on their haggard faces. Just as we were about to board the vessel, the happy sound of a barking dog met our ears, and Holmes and I turned to see the black Labrador, Blackstone, slightly worse for wear, feverishly paddling toward us, its long pink tongue flapping in the salty air.

It looked as happy to see us as we were to see the great dog, again. I moved to pat its side when my hands came away with a palmful of crusted blood as Blackstone let out a whimper of pain. I bent to the site of the wound and noted a series of jagged striations as though it had been viciously swiped by some sharp, many-toothed instrument.

Once we boarded the ship, the captain and crew hastily steered the *Matilda Briggs* into the course that would take us home. The sky was still ominously dark but the rain of volcanic ash and pumice stone had subsided. The deck itself was thick with grey powder that hands were busily sweeping into the sea as the ship pulled its way through the ash-clogged waters.

Portside, I spotted that same unique stretch of land one of the sailors had pointed to as a landmark when we entered the Sumatran region.

"I say, Captain," I shouted, "have you a glass I might borrow?"

I stretched the scope full open and peered in the direction of the jagged dome some fifty kilometers away. I could see its blistered, wrinkled surface and spotted white steam escaping from several fumeroles at the base of the cone. The cone, itself, was now half-hidden by a dense, grey mass of boiling clouds.

"Captain," I said, "there aren't any inhabitants, I pray."

"Uninhabited as far as I know," he shouted.

"Thank God for that."

"Strange, hasn't raised much of a stink in hundreds of years, so they say. And now this."

With the *Matilda Briggs* underway, all that Holmes and I looked forward to was setting foot upon English soil. As a happy footnote to this otherwise sad chapter, the captain agreed to adopt Blackstone as the ship's mascot, and so the great Labrador would come to serve another as faithfully as it had served its fallen master.

"Do you think we saw all there was to see, Holmes?" I asked as the sea slipped past beneath us.

"I doubt it. We must return, Watson, better prepared and better armed. Who knows what other horrors left by that madman, animal or otherwise, still lurk in those steaming jungles? If nothing more, we know the terrain to be infested by those loathsome rodents. Thank God we did not lose any of the survivors to them. They have certainly suffered enough."

"For a lifetime, Holmes, a lifetime."

CHAPTER 20

Return to Baker Street

Never had our landlady's wizened face looked more engaging as when she opened the door on the day of our homecoming and Holmes and I crossed our humble threshold in Baker Street. We had spent months at sea, been threatened by mutinous seamen aboard the *Alice Fair*, come close to being annihilated by a terrifying bomb of unknown origin and been nearly buried under volcanic ash on an unmapped region of Sumatra.

"Mr. Holmes, Mr. Holmes," Mrs. Hudson merrily chanted as she ushered us in, uncharacteristically deferential. To see the entrance to our lodgings once more, the pantry-light shining through the partially open doorway, the bright stair-rods leading upward to our cheery rooms, the rustling curtains of polished cotton: I shamelessly admit that a tear clouded my eye when I saw all this laid before me again.

"Tea, we must have tea," I demanded of Mrs. Hudson, both to help warm my innards and to restore a sense of normality to the household. As she turned toward the pantry, I added, "Oh, Mrs. Hudson, any word?"

"From the young lady, you mean?"

"Yes."

"I'm afraid not, Doctor. Sorry."

"Watson, the hopeless romantic," Holmes chastised with a sigh. "Or should I have said 'hapless?'"

"Holmes!" I protested through my fallen spirits upon Mrs. Hudson's report.

"Very well, a truce," Holmes yielded, then added in a somber tone of voice, "Good as it is to be home, we have dark work still to be done, my man. And a singular question yet hanging in the air."

"I'm afraid I don't follow," I said absently, so overwhelmed was I to find Lucy lost to me still.

"Do you not see that our every move has been watched, somehow transmitted to the nameless fiend over the past several months?"

"Frankly, no," I numbly replied.

"Your thoughts have been elsewhere, my man."

"Perhaps your imagination is overwrought, Holmes," I chided back. "Coincidence, nothing more."

"Tell me this, Watson, how did our foe know we were travelling to his laboratory? How did he know when we would arrive? A predatory agent has been at work here, Watson. And for some time."

"But who could it be, Holmes?"

"Mrs. de Quincey," Mrs. Hudson suddenly announced, peeking through the door. "She's coming up straight away, gentlemen. I informed her that you just arrived."

No sooner had the landlady issued these words than Catherine de Quincey rushed in headed straight in Holmes' direction, her arms open wide to passionately enfold him. Holmes' hands cut her embrace short and pushed her back sternly, his eyes closing to slits as he viewed her as coldly as he might inspect a specimen on a glass before his microscope.

"What is wrong?" she asked.

"You are to leave this house immediately," Holmes decreed.

"I don't understand. Why are you treating me in this fashion?"

"I shall give you ten minutes to secure your belongings and then leave. There is nothing else to be said," declared Holmes in his most frigid manner.

"You do me wrong, sir," Catherine de Quincey boldly rebuked.

"There is nothing more to be said," repeated Holmes.

"And I had come to understand my heart while you were away for so long and on such a terrible mission. I had come to understand that I care for you deeply. Does that mean nothing to you?"

"Come now," Holmes hurrumphed disdainfully, looking Catherine de Quincey up and down. "Heed my injunction and leave this instant," he flatly added, turning his back to her.

Astonishment and grief seemed to struggle for the mastery as the young woman slowly pivoted on the toes of her feet and stepped to the door.

"You do me wrong, Holmes," said Catherine de Quincey, then slipped silently away, down the stairs and out of the life of Sherlock Holmes.

I had come to appreciate the young woman in the most platonic of ways, despite her difficulties, and so I could not agree with Holmes' actions. On the other hand, how many times had the veracity of Holmes' deductions been opaque to me till he described each intermediate point that made a conclusion of his so devastatingly convincing? Would she have been so damnably difficult if her true purpose had been one of espionage? Would it not have better served her purpose to have been more ingratiating? And yet, the rock-steady insusceptibility of Holmes' deductive abilities rose up each time to challenge these doubts of mine.

I found myself with little more to direct at Holmes than, "Are you all right?"

He gave no reply but moved deliberately to his pipe collection and slowly filled one with strong Turkish tobacco, uttering disdainfully under his breath the single phrase, "Cared-for-me."

CHAPTER 21

A Grave Message

The next afternoon found me alone at 221 B, Baker Street, awaiting Holmes' return from visiting Tommy. The young lad was no longer in a coma but still in hospital recovering from his terrible wounds. I knew Holmes held a sincere and biding affection for all members of the irregulars, but especially for young Tommy, one of the first to join his unofficial division of the police force.

I pulled out the copious notes I had scribbled aboard the *Matilda Briggs* and was busy for the next several hours at reconstructing my impressions of our adventure when a note came for me by the last post. I opened it inattentively between sips of tea until I saw the salutation, and my heart nearly leapt from my chest. The handwritten message read:

> Dear John,
>
> Meet me at eleven o'clock tonight at my apartment. I shall explain all then. For heaven's sake, bring your friend, Mr. Holmes, as well. I beg you, do not fail me.
>
> Lucy

A message from Lucy Gates! I had been thinking of her daily since her mysterious disappearance, and she had suddenly reached out to me. Even more, she needed my assistance; here was my opportunity to play rescuing hero to my beloved. But for Lucy to ask for Holmes' aid was prescient of something more sinister than a purloined typewriting machine.

Eventually Holmes entered, announcing, "Watson, Tommy has taken a turn for the worse."

"I am sorry to hear that. I know how much Tommy means to you, Holmes. But he has been fighting weeks of infections and bouts of high fever. I am not surprised."

"That devil!" exclaimed Holmes angrily, pointing in the direction of the sea and beyond to the Sundra Strait from which we had recently returned. "That blackguard has something to do with this. An experiment of his gone monstrously awry."

"Perhaps," I replied, "but allow me to give you some *good* news. Look," passing the note to Holmes.

He gave the note a mere glance.

"There is much on my mind. I do not think I shall join you," declared Holmes.

"Oh, but you must," I insisted. "Can you not see that she is in serious trouble?"

"This is a time for extreme caution, Watson. We are engaged in battling primal forces of evil."

"Lucy Gates has asked for our aid, Holmes. Surely we cannot turn her down."

"Is this her handwriting?" sharply queried Holmes.

"I do not know," I bluntly replied. "I had not even considered—"

"—Have you a sample of her writing?"

"Let me think," I murmured.

"The guest book," exclaimed Holmes, imperiously extending a waiting hand. "She signed it, I believe, the day she came to consult me."

I rummaged amongst Holmes' disorderly stack of papers, notes, a half-finished monograph on the effect of the phases of the moon upon criminal behavior until my fingers found the guest book all visitors were invited to sign and which I handed to him.

Holmes overlapped the note and the guest book where Lucy Gates had signed her name. He reached for the lens with the great ivory handle and minutely inspected the two handwriting samples.

"Hmmm," said Holmes, "the two signatures are not exactly alike."

"Then this note is a fraud? It is not from Lucy?" I asked, troubled and embarrassed.

"You miss my point, Watson," replied Holmes. "They are not identical and so *are* genuine. No one signs his name in exactly the same way twice. To have found precisely matching signatures would have meant a tracing and fraud. But these are just close enough…Yes, my friend, I believe the note to be genuine."

"My God, Holmes, I am relieved."

"And on closer inspection…viewing the haste with which the note was written, the sloppy descenders, the lax loops in the Os and As, and look here, an uncrossed T. Yes, without a doubt, Watson, she is in distress and requires our attention."

"Then you'll come?" I asked hesitantly.

"Looking at the clock, we've not a minute to lose, my friend. Oh, and be so good as to bring that trusty army pistol of yours."

The cab left us at Campton Lane in the midst of a dreary London mist. We scurried up the wet steps to Lucy's front door. Holmes reached for the brass knocker whilst I peered through the frosted window in search of any sign of her presence, comfortingly patting the Eley's through my coat-pocket.

I thought I could see a faint glow of candlelight when Holmes uttered an "aha" to find the door unlocked and slowly swinging inward. Within I faintly beheld Lucy sitting behind a table, the flickering flame of a candle dimly illuminating her oval face, the strain of some ordeal marring the beauty of her regular features. The rest was pitch black save for a glint of light here and there in the room.

"Come in, gentlemen," she whispered with cracked voice. "Forgive me, but I am too weak to receive you."

I followed Holmes, my hand slipping into my coat-pocket and hugging the handle of the Eley's when Lucy blew out the candle!

The darkness of the room grew infinitely deeper as I felt the force of something ramming the back of my head. Holmes, Lucy, the room were swallowed up in the total blackness of unconsciousness.

CHAPTER 22

Lofcadio Hearseborne III

My first impression upon waking was that of bitter, chilling cold. Against my back lay a floor of stone slabs like blocks of ice. By my side Holmes lay unconscious. A dense ammoniac vapour swirled about us amidst blasts of freezing draughts raking the floor in every direction. In the murky distance, I vaguely perceived iron bars such as those of a prison and the licking of a low, dirty-yellow flame far to my left.

Call forth from your imagination the blackest vision of Hades that Danté might have penned: A stomach-churning stench of decay and defecation; a backdrop of faint, unearthly moans; distant scraping as of claws on stone; a slow, steady plop of rank water dripping off rough-hewn cavern walls; reverberations of macabre and sinister cackles.

I was now fully conscious despite the after-effects of what I surmised to be the injection of an alkaloid solution, a hard relentless pounding in my temples and a bitter, metallic taste on the tongue.

A small, brown sewer rat scurried up and comically sniffed my breath with twitching, whiskered, pink nostrils. As though detecting the virulent nature of whatever drug had been introduced into my body, the intelligent little creature suddenly retreated with a frantic gait back into the dark from whence it had come.

Many times in Afghanistan I experienced the somatic effects of fear: The rising heart beat, the dripping palms, the beads of cold sweat on the forehead. I now faced concentrated terror in the extreme. I came to the realization that my hands and feet were bound with plaster-drenched rags!

Looking over to Holmes, I saw that he had been restrained in the same fashion. We were utterly helpless, Holmes and I, whatever arcane knowledge of knots he possessed to no avail. My pistol and its fate now crossed my mind, and I knew that the service-revolver must have been lost to whomever perpetrated the assault.

Then Lucy's betrayal came flooding to mind, and I cursed the day that I met her. What had I done to turn her so against me that she should have led Holmes and me to this nightmare?

I called out, "Holmes, Holmes!" only to hear the sound of my hoarse voice echoing back. Then I noted that Holmes had been ill treated, an angry welt upon his forehead. I suddenly feared that he might even be in a coma from which he would not awaken.

I tried again to rouse him.

"Holmes, wake up!" I cried. "Wake up!"

A low moan escaped Holmes. His eyelids fluttered, and with relief I saw that he was stirring to consciousness.

"Holmes," I said again, "for God's sake, wake up."

With a jolt, Holmes snapped to attention, his eyes suddenly sharply alert.

"What have we here, Watson?" he asked pointedly, reviewing the surroundings and the manner in which we were bound.

Raw panic seemed to overcome Holmes' expression. I could only imagine that he suddenly foresaw the inexorable conclusion as vividly as any of his past deductions. We were about to face our own deaths!

Suddenly a formidable figure emerged from the inky blackness, another form much the smaller trailing behind like a stray dog. "Son of a whore," bellowed the large form to the small. "Get back where you belong! Must you make after my every step!"

The immense figure climaxed the verbal assault with a swift kick to the creature's rump. With dog-like yelps, the frail form limped off in the direction of the pale, flickering light. The huge figure drew closer to us with a porcine waddle, stopping a few meters away and attempting a clumsy bow from the waist.

"Mr. Holmes, Dr. Watson," the form declared. "A distinct pleasure."

"I regret that I cannot return the compliment," Holmes sharply retorted.

"Allow me to introduce myself. I am Lofcadio Hearseborne III. Please consider my home as yours." He made a sweeping gesture with a ham-sized hand that wafted the foul air before my nostrils. "As you see, I have made every effort to make your visit a comfortable one."

With these words he exploded in a wild chortle that brought him to his knees, coughing and gasping for breath. He arose, wiping spittle from his mouth, and exclaimed, "The curse of age, gentlemen. My one consolation, like yours, is my work. The work of a lifetime."

"A strange concept of work," uttered Holmes, "pillaging homes like a common street thug, savaging unknown numbers of innocents, destroying all who stand in your way." He spat these words out with a vehemence that called forth to me the loss of Captain Paulsen, his crew and the nameless victims of the *Alice Fair's* steerage class.

Hearseborne replied, "My apologies, one finds it difficult to get good help these days, mistaking mere typewriting machines for a refinement, a delicacy of engineering beyond their imaginations. I have punished them well, do not fret." Suddenly, he boomed into the dark, "Chair!"

The same sorry creature came wheeling an enormous arm-chair on rollers, then scurried off much like the brown rat that had sniffed my breath. Hearseborne's Falstaffian form sank deeply into the leather seat.

"Let us come to the heart of the matter, Mr. Holmes," he uttered with eyes malevolently twinkling. "Perhaps for the first time in your life, you are fearful, even terrified. And why? Because of the very powers that have served you so ably in the past and that have threatened the perpetuation of my enterprises…till now, Mr. Holmes."

Suddenly he slapped his massive thigh triumphantly. "I know that you see the inevitability of your death as clearly as you see the implications of red clay upon the sole of a shoe. I find something in this too delicious for words.

"Confide in me, Mr. Holmes. How come you to your incredible deductions?"

"That, Hearseborne, you may purchase with our freedom," Holmes flippantly responded.

"I think not. I know the answer you would give, some nonsense as to analytic powers. You see, I am a student of the occult, and your case intrigues me. I believe you share Nostradamus' gifts. I have often wondered, might his revelations be attributed to skills much like yours, only elevated to an exponential degree of refinement? The premise transfixes my imagination."

He wiped the sweat that had beaded on his forehead, continuing, "You see how fertile a mind I possess, gentlemen? It never stops seeking the truth, analyzing facts, formulating grand theories. It is a curse as much as a blessing, for I can never rest. I see humanity as through a pane of glass, an observer, never a participant. Love, marriage, children: These matters are for the innocents, the foolish masses, the faceless *bourgeoisie*. But I stray, for in truth I wished to thank you, Mr. Holmes."

"Thank me?"

"Yes, you have bestowed upon me the magnificent gift of confession. It is good for the soul, I understand. You see, none shall save you, Mr. Holmes. To one such as you with no future, I may divulge the most intimate of secrets, knowing they shall travel no further than these quarters."

Hearseborne bent directly over Holmes, dripping his foul sweat upon my friend's face. "For your kindness, may I reciprocate in kind with some small favor, sir?"

"A drink of water for us both would suffice," Holmes hoarsely replied.

"Water!" bellowed Hearseborne into the darkness.

Momentarily, another horrid, misshapen creature frantically shuffled forward, a crystal goblet brimming with water in its gnarled hands. It had the misfortune to stumble within a few steps of me, sending the goblet to shatter by my cheek and splashing water onto the stone floor half hidden in folds of grey mist.

With nary a hesitation, Hearseborne set upon the wretch, kicking it mercilessly in the ribs and face, spewing it with epithets of such vile nature that decency prohibits my repeating them within this account. The pitiable beast begged with hoarse lamentations for him to cease, raising its bloodied, twisted hands in supplication.

"Very well," bellowed Hearseborne after a moment of reflection. "You are in luck. Mr. Holmes and Dr. Watson's presence to-night has put me in a kindly frame of mind. Get out of my sight!"

Unable to stand on its fractured limbs, the pitiable creature pulled itself away by bleeding, deformed hands. "Forgive him, gentlemen, his clumsiness. One of my less successful endeavours."

Hearseborne caught the horror in my eyes as my worst suspicions were now confirmed. "Oh yes, Dr. Watson, human experimentation, human vivisection. Do not be naive. They are essential, you see. When one plays with the elemental powers of the universe, a life here or there means less than the falling of a leaf. By good fortune, God has provided me with such bounty—and in so many colours, black, brown, yellow—that an occasional disappearance is not to be missed. As much as I treasure all life, with reluctance I must sacrifice a few for the benefit of the many."

With these words, Hearseborne bent over a shard of the splintered crystal strewn before me. My heart leapt to my throat as the dim light traced its razor-sharp edges till Hearseborne gently tipped the gleaming fragment to my lips and allowed a tiny stream of water to trickle down my parched throat, then moved to Holmes and repeated his benevolent gesture.

"Since I have afforded you such peace of mind," Holmes brashly countered with renewed strength, "be so kind as to disclose the precise nature of your experiments. I have my theories, of course, but prefer corroboration directly from the author."

"My plan exactly, sir," said Hearseborne, withdrawing a panatela from a golden, hammered cigar-case. "Mr. Holmes, my entire life has been a search for the truth.

"I grew up devouring all I could lay hands on pertaining to natural history, beginning with Pliny and Aristotle, moving on from their quaint philosophies to more contemporary view-points. The intellectual superiority with which I was blessed allowed me to separate wheat from chaff, from what De Maillet and Buffon had to say as to our origins, refusing to be betrayed by their inexcusable lapses in common sense whilst allowing myself inspiration in the few words of truth which their faulty voices whispered in my ear.

"I early on determined Africa as Man's place of origin. With these very hands, Mr. Holmes, I dug out of the dust of that continent remains of our ancestors that would bring forth a collective gasp of astonishment from the scientific community. From there I glimpsed the grand plan of Nature which passed unnoticed by lesser men, including that ape, Charles Darwin.

"The small-minded, timid weasel! He hasn't the courage to forthrightly proclaim his views. Like a buffoon, holding hands with the Church, he dances round the heart of the matter: That man has evolved, as have all other plants and animals on this earth.

"And then his ridiculous theory of pangenesis, a warmed-over version of archaic nonsense with miniature copies of body parts—gemmules, he calls them—floating about in our bloodstream, recording our experiences and gathering in our gonads whence we pass on this wonderful, acquired knowledge to our offspring. Contemptible drivel! One step away from believing in homunculi. I knew that some other dynamic must be at work: A *particulate* theory.

"Toward the funding of this pursuit, I applied the most modern of administrative concepts to criminal enterprises on a vast scale including prostitution, large-scale burglary, white slavery, pornography, opium-trading and other age-old, cherished institutions. If you could but observe, Mr. Holmes, the elegance of my masterly control over the criminal activity underway in this city, not to mention other countries and continents, even you—yes, you, Mr. Holmes—should be impressed. Dare I claim that the returns from my underground economy rival the gross national profits of many a nation, including her Majesty's empire?"

"There is a delightful Americanism, Hearseborne," I said, looking round, "To the effect of not putting up much of a front."

"*Touché*, Dr. Watson, *touché!* But then all is perspective, is it not? Heaven and hell, freedom and imprisonment: One man's concept of beauty is another's object of derision. To be frank, I prefer the bowels of the earth to London's poisonous fumes. The heady perfumes of her subterranean fauna and flora are to me infinitely preferable to the saccharine oppressiveness of Hyde Park's blossoming flowers!

"Above I am too far removed from the mysteries of Death, though that veiled form approaches each of us ever closer by the day. In this sanctuary where I have chosen to exile myself, I stand but a heartbeat from my next plane of existence, gentlemen. I am by Death's side observing his handiwork, succumbing to his offerings. Who can say that the exhilarating fragrance of decay is less than the banal stench of birth? This is my home of choice, sir, not of need.

"Oh, gentlemen! Surely, you must appreciate the grandeur of my efforts. If only you knew the vast network I have constructed across the scientific community to effect the next step, a living web vibrating its alarm with each new idea, caught as though some poor, hapless intellectual fly.

"Even you, Mr. Holmes, could not guess the scope of my army of readers, devouring each monograph in or out of print, exalted or obscure. The treatises of the Nine Unknown Men alone would take an ordinary man a lifetime to digest."

"Then the Nine Unknown Men do exist?" Holmes bluntly asked, genuine interest in his voice.

"*Did,* Mr. Holmes, did. Until each suffered an unfortunate accident, long before your dear Darwin began receiving those threatening messages. By good fortune, I acquired their books of clandestine scientific facts, which have been of occasional benefit to my mission."

"I should be most interested in seeing them, Hearseborne," said Holmes.

"Oh, to be sure," he remarked with a smirk, "and to discover the location of my private library. No, no, Mr. Holmes, I think not. I am disappointed: A bit transparent for one with a reputation for cleverness.

"However, would you gentlemen care to see my study?"

"Delighted," I replied, stunned at the speed with which Hearseborne leapt from subject to subject.

"But we are at a disadvantage, sir," added Holmes.

"Ah, are you suggesting I have my aides break your bonds, Mr. Holmes, and say, shackle you with regulation bracelets?"

"I leave it to your good judgment."

"Of course." Hearseborne tapped the tips of his sausage-sized fingers together, then chuckled to himself. "Mr. Holmes, I am aware of your extremely fascinating little monograph, *On The Usage of The Art of Escapism and Prestidigitation in Criminology.* Ah, if only you could survive long enough to entertain during one of my gala celebrations."

His great brows drew down into dense furrows. "For now, the bonds remain, gentlemen. I shall have my colleagues assist you into my study where I am sure you shall be more at ease."

CHAPTER 23

The Akashic Record

Two burly men with gun-coloured faces carried us over their shoulders through the murky entrails of Hearseborne's subterranean haunt. I surmised that we were following the course of London's Walbrook River whose black waters churned with a low rumbling toward their rendezvous with the Thames.

Hearseborne turned round to say, "It may be of interest to you gentlemen that we are presently under the Bank of England." He pointed a stubby thumb upward to the coal-coloured canopy of rock high above our heads, my eyes tracing the progress of a small tunnel already coarsely under excavation.

Soon the cavern smoothed and opened into an anachronistic vision: A ballroom-sized, regally-appointed interior; deep-blue carpet of the most luxuriant quality; gold lamps draped with gleaming baccarat crystal; plush, over-sized arm-chairs of well-worn Moroccan leather. By an enormous tapestry of shimmering silken thread bearing an intricate Oriental motif Holmes and I were rudely flung.

"I see that you place a high value on owning beautiful objects, Hearseborne," Holmes harshly said after regaining his wind. I suddenly noticed Holmes wiggling his right fingers behind the small of his back, so as—I deduced—to catch my eye. It was then that I noticed the long, jagged crack along the plaster binding Holmes' arms, caused, I surmised, by the force of his fall. With great effort I withheld the impulse to beam triumphantly. He continued, "I have in mind the lives of seventy-two men and women.

"This tapestry is strikingly familiar to me. I recall the Oxfordshire Music Hall's disastrous fire which claimed seventy-two lives two years past; the theatre had proudly displayed just such a work of art. I note, too, a row of its velvet chairs against the other wall and the slightly charred legs of several of the chairs."

"You have an eye, Mr. Holmes," replied Hearseborne, "indeed you do. Yes, a magnificent structure burnt beyond recognition, a tragedy of Biblical proportion. The solvent I used produced a flame of unexpectedly high temperature.

"But what a stroke of genius to have devised such a project, Mr. Holmes: To have placed the correct number of my men in the audience, waiting patiently to assist me with split-second timing: To have calculated the optimal quantity of solvent to achieve the desired result: To have arranged the canisters in points throughout the hall with mathematical precision to burn what I wanted burnt whilst giving my men time to rescue what I desired salvaged."

With these words he fondled the silk curtain with vulgar sensuality. "I suppose you have already admired the Rembrandt—"

"—and the Vermeer. Missing several years from the Vatican collection. However, I'm sorry to be the one to inform you. That bust, the small study by Flauvert: It is a fake, Hearseborne."

"Fake?" he cried out, lunging at the terra cotta. This he scrutinized as a pantry maid might inspect a melon for ripeness, passing the bust from hand to hand, twirling it between his fingers and squinting his smoldering eyes.

"The work is obviously inferior to Flauvert's technique, Hearseborne," Holmes continued, deliciously, snobbishly cruel. "Possibly executed by one of his students, I should think."

"Yes, I see it now," he grumbled to himself, spittle flying from his mouth. "I'll have no spurious art in my collection," he roared and flung the work to shatter against the wall by my side.

Hearseborne filled a goblet with brandy from a crystal decanter and greedily gulped down the amber liqueur, his breast still heaving with the ferocity of his anger.

"I recall an aphorism, something concerning a 'silk purse and a sow's ear,'" Holmes said derisively. "In the end, I see that living with art—even at the cost of innocent lives—cannot endow a Philistine with the discrimination of an aesthete."

"You take chances, Holmes. Art for me is an escape from petty minds such as yours and Scotland Yard's and others seeking my destruction!"

Holmes declared, "Here, here. One fact I know for certain, that you are not above corrupting young women in your quest for absolute power."

"I have found that women possess a remarkable talent for corrupting themselves, Mr. Holmes," countered Hearseborne. "Consider the young lady in your life, the affable Catherine de Quincey."

Holmes' face flushed when her name issued from Hearseborn's vile lips. "Then you *do* know of the young woman in question?" Holmes asked.

"I know of everyone in your life, Mr. Holmes. She is captivating, is she not? You are a fortunate young man. Oh, and Dr. Watson," he added, withdrawing a thin manuscript from a bureau drawer, "I believe this belongs to you."

He threw before me my essay, tattered and dog-eared, regarding my feminine ideal, a long-lost relic from my days at university.

"What is the meaning of this?" I hotly queried, to which I received but a vulgar chortle from Hearseborne.

"Is there no depth to which you would not sink, sir?" cried Holmes.

With these words, Hearseborne waddled up to us and moved his massive head, with its wild mane of white hair, inches from my friend, Hearseborne's burning eyes set upon Holmes for what seemed an eternity.

"The great Sherlock Holmes," he spat out. "Not even the filth of my humble domicile soils his immaculate self.

"Do you know what I perceive as the next essential step in the evolution, if you will, of crime?" Hearseborne paused for a response, but Holmes gave him none.

"The ingestion—forgive me, Mr. Holmes, I said ingestion, not injection—of narcotics." Hearseborne briefly paused for a reaction. "Have you an opinion upon the subject? I see by your silence that you prefer to just say 'no.' Let me put it to you in this way, then. You enjoy your white powder, do you not?"

With the question put so bluntly to Holmes he seemed to squirm uneasily where he lay.

"I have it on good authority," pressed Hearseborne, "that you have been known to enjoy a seven percent solution two times, on occasion, three times a day. Is that not so?"

Hearseborne moved his massive face an inch from Holmes, repeating the words with a terrible hiss, "Is that not so!"

"My private life is no concern of yours, Hearseborne," retorted my friend.

Hearseborne gathered Holmes' collar in his massive hands and violently shook him, bellowing, "No concern of mine…Has it ever occurred to you, Mr. Sherlock Holmes, who it is—"

"No!" Holmes protested, it seemed to me more to himself than to Hearseborne. "No, do not say it!"

"—who it is that risks all to serve you, to provide you with—"

"Say no more, I beg of you," cried Holmes.

"—to provide you with your precious cocaine? It is I, Mr. Holmes, I, Lofcadio Hearseborne III."

I heard a low, sustained moan issuing from what I could only describe as the very pit of Holmes' being.

"You," Hearseborne continued, "have had no small part in my enterprises!"

Holmes' moan rose into a long, protracted wail of utter anguish. I could only imagine with what force the revelation that Holmes should have in any measure collaborated with this loathsome creature came crushing down upon my poor friend.

How came he, Holmes must have been asking himself, not to appreciate the consequences of his base actions? He who could trace the minute and nearly invisible trail of cause and effect through all other venues of life? Holmes' spirit seemed to wither before my eyes and hopelessness to engulf him totally.

"No matter, Mr. Holmes," Hearseborne continued in a cavalier fashion. "We all have our weaknesses. I am the most forgiving of men. And I still mean to have you hear my confession. I long for an intellectual exchange, compassed round as I am by mindless beasts fit only to perform the menial tasks I demand of them. But in your presence, I burn to discuss my great work in the knowledge that you may appreciate the full import of my disclosures."

With an oversized hand, Hearseborne forced Holmes' chin up so that their eyes locked.

"I have made the giant leap, Holmes. I have formulated a grand theory, from snatches of knowledge here and there, from the babblings of a pathetic old man named Charles Darwin and an idiot abbot and all the other small-minded men who have stood at the brink but had not the courage to delve into that sea of ultimate discovery laid before them. I alone have discovered the secrets of Life!"

He refilled his goblet and sank into the largest of the surrounding chairs. In my own despair and in my growing discomfort, his words ran one into the other, ringing dull and hollow in my ear.

Hearseborne drew in another long draught of his brandy with the pretense of savouring its bouquet whilst Holmes, his head bowed, continued a series of doleful moans.

"I have gone beyond a particulate theory of heredity. I have discovered the fundamental building block of life, Holmes: A molecule that I imagine duplicating itself in miraculous fashion, uncoiling to become life anew. And within this molecule the particles of information that make you, Mr. Holmes, a consulting detective and me, well, all that I am. Particles of life, waiting for me to shuffle at my will, to fulfill my ultimate destiny, to take my place among the pantheon of Gods!"

Even in the depth of my despair, my blood froze as I heard these terrible words booming from Hearseborne's lips. Rant as he may, I knew that they were not hollow conceits but declarations of determined, twisted genius.

"Have you any conception of the power I now hold in my hands, Holmes?" Hearseborne brought forth from his coat-pocket a gilt-edged deck of playing cards.

"Consider these pasteboards, Mr. Holmes. As easily as I shuffle them, I may now shuffle the particles of Life, mine to manipulate as Nature—or God, if that be your other opiate of choice—once did. I reshuffle the particles of an organism and create the perfect beast of burden, domesticated from inception, willing to labor till it drops, subsisting on the meanest quantity of feed and water.

"I take a creature, *Rhizomys sumatrensis,* the giant rat of Sumatra, a vulgar beast from the stinking jungles of Indonesia, and develop a breed of vermin at my beck and call, hungering to tear my enemies to shreds with but a snap of my fingers. Shall I demonstrate? Not yet? Very well. Perhaps I shall wait to practice upon Lucy Gates."

"Lucy Gates!" I exclaimed, my outrage rising with renewed contempt for the beast before me. Lucy Gates, I thought to myself: the young woman in whom I had placed such affection and concern.

"What have you done with her?" I demanded.

"Forget her, Dr. Watson. Once I have no need of her, she shall become a plaything for my pets."

"Damn you!" I boomed, straining at my constraints. "May you burn in Hell!"

"Such passion, Doctor, for one who betrayed you. Highly commendable," praised Hearseborne with honeyed sarcasm. "By the by, does either of you recall the Latin of your halcyon school days? The word *ratus*, for example, as in rat? It means 'to gnaw,' good Doctor, 'to gnaw.'

"But allow me to continue my confession to Mr. Holmes. I intend, you see, to create a community of criminals with all adaptive characteristics intact, adept at scrambling walls, listening to the subtlest of tumblers falling into place within the vaults of the great banks of the world.

"To create a race of warriors: Impervious to pain, dedicated to fulfilling my every order, ready and willing—dare I say, eager—to spill their blood in pursuit of my most trivial caprice. No sex drive till I bid them procreate. No stunting ethics. No squeamish reluctance to murder or to torture man, woman, child for the sake of my larger vision.

"By manipulation of the particles of life that I have discovered, I shall bring forth from the laboratory perfect replicas of myself in any quantity I so choose. Immortality, Mr. Holmes!" And then Hearseborne gave forth a queer, high-pitched snigger as he added, "Who's to say, Holmes, that the being standing before you isn't the product of such a convoluted experiment, eh?"

My ears pricked at this troubling, cryptic remark, but the timing of our discussion had a life of its own. With quavering voice, Holmes asked, "You truly intend to alter the course of evolution to your purpose?"

"I am greatly disappointed, Mr. Holmes. You have missed the point. Evolution is dead. *I* have murdered it!

"And I have inherited its ultimate destiny. I have become Executioner of the Useless and of the Unfit! I am become Death, Holmes, the shatterer of Worlds!

"Shall I disclose my greater ambitions?"

"Pray continue," Holmes sardonically replied.

Hearseborne now moved his great mass but an inch over Holmes, Hearseborne's sweat splattering my friend's face and his hot, rancid breath fanning across us in odious waves.

"I intend to create a species of bacteria with but one function: To scourge the world of the Jew, lay waste to adult and child alike and bring to an end, finally, his parasitic reign on the commerce of this land! To that end, my rats shall do double duty. Are you a student of medieval history, Mr. Holmes, as I am? The Black Death decimated half of Europe, but that was nothing compared to what I have planned."

Holmes shook his head in disbelief as Hearseborne continued.

"I shall develop yet another strain targeted at the Negro population, save those I choose to reserve as my personal attendants—as did the great Emperors of a glorious, nearly forgotten past. You see that I stick at nothing."

Hearseborne began foaming at the mouth in a burst of excitement, spraying the air with his spittle and flaying the fetid air with broad, frenzied sweeps of his arms.

"I cannot believe," Holmes declared, "that anyone, even you, Hearseborne, should wish to decimate an entire race of man."

"As you shall see, Holmes, Watson, I am but a step away from all these achievements!"

With these words, Hearseborne grasped the wall by his massive frame and with a great grunt slid aside a stone partition to reveal a secreted grotto. A soft metallic clattering suddenly filled the air, the sound emanating from a chest-sized, cage-like structure resting on a hefty side-table by the edge of the recess.

In a chair to its left, bound in rough strips of cloth and coarse braids of rope, her screams constricted by a tightly applied bandanna across her mouth and with terror in her tear-stained eyes, squirmed Lucy Gates. Her blouse had been torn, exposing her throat and upper arm. From the corner of my eye, I caught a startled expression on Holmes' face; he must have been as surprised as I to find Lucy in so compromised a position. Seeing her in this state melted away any reservation I had about her, and I understood immediately that she must have been compelled under some heinous threat to lead us to the beast before us.

Lucy looked at me pleadingly, pathetically, but I was immobile in my constraints. When she found Holmes' dilemma echoing mine, hopelessness seemed to engulf her wholly on realizing the folly of escape. Feelings of guilt and shame arose within me in my impotence, and I turned my attention back to the recess.

Great, rough-hewn granite steps led up from the floor of the grotto to a stone pedestal upon which rested an immense object. I would needs call it a book—the largest ever upon which I had laid eyes—yet in my growing fatigue it seemed not so much a book as an apparition, an incorporeal entity spewing a fiery, shimmering glow in every direction. Neither did the mysterious volume seem to rest upon the pedestal so much as to hover just above it.

And yet I would have sworn that the tome had substantial weight. In my stupor, it seemed to dip slightly now and then, grinding the stone beneath to a powder that cascaded to the floor in a fine stream. Ask me not how, but the mystic volume appeared to exist concurrently in two parallel worlds, the corporeal and the metaphysical.

Massive was the volume's width, surely spanning the greater part of two yards. The tome's very shape appeared to alter before my eyes, one moment mimicking the likeness of an ancient scroll and then with a shudder, unfolding into the form of an immense leather-bound treatise, electric blue sparks seemingly tracing the ragged edges of its sheets and filling the dark, craggy recess with an icy, flickering glow.

As Hearseborne ascended the coarse steps to the treatise, he turned to Holmes to ask, "Are you familiar, Mr. Holmes, with the Akashic record?"

The shock of seeing Lucy Gates must have rallied Holmes from his despair, for I saw a fire burning once more in his eyes. He gave me a wink as if to say, "The game is afoot, *again*, Watson!"

"I have confronted the phrase," Holmes replied with renewed strength in his voice. "I recall that the Akashic record is considered a metaphysical concept, a source of all knowledge past, present and future that only the most accomplished of mystics may attain in their quest for ultimate truth."

"Up to a point, Mr. Holmes, you are well informed," blasted Hearseborne, who towered above us atop the stone slabs, a priest of Hades before his profane altar.

"I, too, believed the Akashic record to be a mere construct until my insatiable curiosity led me to discover that the physical record had been secreted within the great Alexandrian library, that it had been rescued from Caesar's flames by a devout, clandestine sect fanatically devoted to preserving the ancient text at any cost. Many of its devotees met a horrible, fiery death attempting to preserve the singular volume, but to their credit the record was rescued intact. I traced its journey down through the centuries to its last hiding place in catacombs deep beneath Jerusalem, and behold—the Akashic record!"

Hearseborne caressingly smoothed the top of the Akashic record with the palms of his ham-sized hands, then tried to turn the volume's leaves. In my near delirium, the pages appeared to slip and slide from his fingers as though evading his touch, not so much pages of a book as wafers of pure transcendental light. With determined effort, he managed to turn a leaf and then another, leaf upon leaf, each page he managed to swing round softly crackling whilst vivid, blue sparks danced, it seemed to me, along its gilt edges.

"Inscribed within," Hearseborne continued, "is the history of the cosmos, its birth and its death. All events and their instigators from the most profound to the lowliest are contained within the Akashic record.

"Even your pathetic history, Mr. Holmes, and yours, Dr. Watson, may be found within the weave of its cosmic fabric. Much of its contents I have been able to read directly and make use of toward my ambitions.

"But I uncovered a startling secret of the Akashic record. Its most profound knowledge had been diabolically encrypted into the very text itself. Little of true value can be deciphered by mere mortals, even by one as gifted as I.

"It was then that I hit upon the idea of devising a calculating machine to aid in its translation and began recruiting engineers for its development. Happily, I came across the work of one Charles Babbage through an associate in the Royal Astronomical Society and learnt of Babbage's attempts to build such a device of his own.

"The common perception was that Babbage designed many such machines on paper but never constructed a working model. My research, however, confirmed he had built at least one such device he called an Analytical Engine; in appearance it somewhat resembled a large typewriting machine. My colleagues began a focused search throughout greater London to 'borrow' any machines resembling the treasure.

"Then Providence brought me great news. Babbage had trained a distant relative—the young actress before you whom you know as Lucy Gates—in its most intimate secrets. For safekeeping upon his death, Babbage quietly willed it to Miss Gates, a young ineffectual woman no one would suspect as the caretaker of such a marvelous instrument. And now there she sits, eager to come to my aid should I require some little assistance.

"Congratulations, gentlemen," Hearseborne continued, glancing at his pocket watch, "your timing is most fortuitous. You are about to witness a singular event, the precise moment in Time when my wondrous Analytical Engine divulges the final information I require of the Akashic record to complete my plans. I have put the machine to work for a fortnight and the results should be at hand at any moment."

Hearseborne waved over two henchmen and gleefully ordered that they prepare a celebratory banquet in honor of his upcoming triumph. Upon his curt dismissal, they scurried off with bowed heads into the darkness.

A bell-like clang suddenly sang out from the machine indicating some state of readiness. With twitching fingers, Hearseborne awkwardly moved several long levers on the side of the engine causing inner cogs and wheels to spin furiously and creating a rising din of metallic clattering. The instant Hearseborne turned to make some adjustment to the device, Holmes smacked his wiry legs smartly against the ground, creating fissures in their plaster bindings.

Lucy Gates, surprised by his unexpected maneuver, locked her eyes upon Holmes. With Hearseborne's attention still occupied, I frowned, grimaced and sternly shook my head at her, lest Hearseborne should catch the object of her attentions. But her gaze remained pinned upon Holmes, and my heart sank even as I awaited an opportunity to mimic his actions.

The clattering abruptly stopped. Hearseborne paused before the device, a quivering hand to his heart.

"What now, Miss Gates?" he softly inquired, his eyes nervously running across the complex maze of shafts, gears and pulleys. To her silence, he repeated, "What now?" with deeper, threatening timbre. Pulling her head back by a handful of her hair, he hissed, "Surely, we don't wish another demonstration of my powers of persuasion, Miss Gates, now do we?"

Straining at my bonds, I saw Lucy whip her face away from his, tears streaming from her eyes. With quivering lips, she whispered something under her breath. Hearseborne triumphantly reared back his head, his white mane tossing to and fro, and barked a coarse laugh.

His forefinger circled above a small red key until he caught the smallest, hesitant nod of confirmation from Lucy, who then lowered her head, I surmised, in shame. With a press of the key, Hearseborne caused the device to leap again to clattering life. Holmes sharply flung his arms against the floor with a queer, flailing motion of his body. In a few moments, the great machine fell silent, and a tongue of white paper appeared in a slot at the base of the calculating engine.

Hearseborne tremulously pulled the strip of paper from the slot. With eyes dull and lifeless as the black discs of a shark, he studied the results with gravest intensity when he let loose the deepest, most mournful wail ever I heard issue from the depths of the soul.

"The record shows, Mr. Holmes," he disclosed with quavering voice, the paper tape slipping from his numb fingers, "that I am…too ahead of my time.

"Too ahead of my time!" he began savagely chanting.

"For all my research, all my brilliance, the plans I so carefully constructed, I suffer now as Tantalus suffers in the bowels of Hell. For I am locked in this dread century with its clumsy technology. I am to be denied my dearest ambitions. *That* is what the cursed book has to say.

"It spells out, you see, the limits of my century! Give me fifty years, a hundred years more and the techniques I need are mine to command. But here, at the end of this wretched century, I find my instruments too blunt, my forceps, scalpels too coarse.

"Damned, cursed fate!" he vociferously protested to the heavens, beating at the foul air with his great fists.

Every object within reach now became a deadly instrument of his rage hurtled through the air with abandon. Crystal goblets splintered. A golden candelabra twisted into a grotesque tangle of metallic arms as it clanged dully against rock some meters away from Holmes. A marble bust shattered into dagger-like shards before me. Wildly, Hearseborne blindly hurtled object upon object to every corner of the room.

Spent and heaving asthmatically, Hearseborne ran to the alcove and sprang upon Babbage's machine with animal ferocity. With one mighty lunge he lifted the device high above his head and tossed it, clattering gears and all, in the direction of the mighty volume at the top of the granite steps.

Seemingly alight in a blue flame, the great Akashic record shifted off its centre, its crisp, translucent leaves flapping noisily in the air. It was then that Holmes somehow flipped to his feet, shook off the calcified bonds from his extremities with lightning speed and furiously propelled the other splintered, plaster shell over his head and in Hearseborne's direction. My friend instantly snapped to a fighting stance, fists making small powerful circles before him! Hearseborne moved to lift the still clattering device as a metallic bludgeon when Holmes, spring-like, hurtled himself into the air, a missile of deadly force, and planted his sinewy right leg dead against Hearseborne's mighty chest. His massive form stumbled back, arms gesticulating wildly, and crashed into the stone steps below the Akashic record.

The great book vibrated, teetered precariously on the edge of its massive pedestal for a fraction of a second, then tumbled down the stone steps with ear-splitting thuds in Hearseborne's direction.

He thrust up both arms in a pitiably futile act of self-protection as the tome crashed down upon him. One last mournful dirge feebly rose from the lips of Lofcadio Hearseborne III as the oppressive sheaves of the Akashic record burst his lungs and snuffed out the life from his gargantuan frame.

CHAPTER 24

The Giant Rats of Sumatra

How something so apparently insubstantial as the great book had concurrently the weight to crush Hearseborne I cannot explain. But before my weary eyes I saw the mighty volume tumble down the steps to press the life out of his massive body.

Now Holmes set to work freeing me from my constraints. Suddenly, one of Hearseborne's henchmen lumbered out from the darkness and clubbed the back of my friend's head with a wooden bludgeon. Holmes collapsed to the ground. The blackguard whipped out a revolver, pointing it menacingly in my direction.

"Kill our master, will you?" he spat out vehemently, hate burning in slitted eyes. "First you two blokes, then the bird."

Looking over my bonds with a smirk, he grunted, "Guess I've no need for this, eh?" and carelessly tossed the pistol to the ground. With a start and a surge of indignation, I realized that the villain had been unwittingly threatening me with my very own trusty Eley's and that it now lay by the blackguard's feet and but a scant meter out of reach, though it may as well have been half a world away.

He lifted me as though I were a rag doll, and we coursed through tortuous catacombs edged in blue, smoky light. A glint of the bars which I had earlier noticed reappeared along with the frightful squealing to which I had first awakened.

As we gained on the cell, I realized that it was, in fact, one of a row of enormous cages whose hideous inhabitants, the giant rats from Sumatra, teemed upon each other, red glowing eyes ever more aware of our steady approach.

I was now close enough to sniff their filthy, grease-matted, red-orange pelts. With horror I observed that—caught up in a bestial frenzy of appetite—the rats had set upon one another with cannibalistic gusto. Numbers of them carried severed tails or sharp-clawed, rust-coloured paws in their drooling jaws. The hellish beasts clumsily slid in pools of their own blood, driving them on to ever wilder orgies of torn flesh and shattered bone.

As the scoundrel tossed me within arm's length of one of the latched cage doors, I noted something incredible. Despite the rats' frenzied bloodlust, some memory of unspeakable cruelty on the henchman's part sent the loathsome, mastiff-sized beasts clamouring over and under each other in quest of the corner of the cage farthest away.

"Now for the other bloke," the henchman grunted, disappearing into the blackness to collect Holmes. The moment he left, the pack of beasts, a mass of blood-stained teeth and rust-coloured muzzles, scurried toward me, and I wiggled my way a safe distance from the cage door.

When the horde again retreated in a wave of matted red hair to the far corner of the cage, I knew that the blackguard was about to reappear. He stepped into a bleak pool of light and flung Holmes from his shoulder to land hard by my side with a low groan.

"I hain't fed 'em yet," said the villain with a grim smirk. The beasts scurried back, leaving a great gap between themselves and the metal door rattling with their frenzied commotion.

"Know what them goes for first?" he hissed, withdrawing a large rusty key from his vest pocket and vacantly fumbling at the keyhole as he searched my eyes for a trace of fear.

"The eyes. They love them eyes. The way they laps at that purple goo, like it was honey-sweet."

I felt my heart stop when the key slid in place, finding the tumblers with a sharp, metallic report, and the lock noisily sprang open.

Now he set to work at the rusted door, stubbornly resisting his violent tugs with a horrid grating of metal on stone. One of the larger, more aggressive rats suddenly scrambled forward from the cowering pack and threw itself into the widening chasm between door and cage, its bristling, gore-besmirched muzzle corkscrewing forward with savage fury in my direction.

"Well, hain't that somethin'?" the villain barked. "Maybe I'll just watch that thing eat the top of your 'ead off."

He grabbed me by the lapels and dragged me within an inch of the loathsome beast when I heard a loud crack and saw the thug clutch at his crimson throat.

His body fell atop me with a ghastly gurgling sound and wedged itself like a human dam within the gaping cage door, inviting the hellish hoard to feast upon the grisly repast.

I turned sharply to a billowing cloud of grey smoke. The blur of a form moved through the acrid haze. Then pallid, simian features emerged, a pistol clenched in white, gnarled fingers.

"Sir Charles!" I exclaimed.

Darwin stood before me, the revolver still smoking in his trembling right hand, a cane in the other.

"Can I believe my eyes?" I bellowed. "Holmes, wake up! It's Darwin!" I babbled, "Charles Darwin!"

The pistol's report and my ravings had worked to rouse Holmes. "Yes, my friend," he groggily agreed as he slowly came to, shaking his battered head and rubbing his neck.

"Now to free you of those bonds!" exclaimed Darwin, tossing the pistol aside.

As Darwin attacked my constraints with the heavily knobbed walking stick, I looked round to witness what remained of the wretch's quivering hulk. With the grotesque pitching and jerking of a nightmarish marionette, it was drawn ever deeper into the cage by the churning maelstrom of red, grizzled fur and flashing yellow incisors.

One of the rats suddenly abandoned its repast, leaping past the top of the cage door to sink its teeth into the shank of my leg through the set plaster. I felt a sharp stinging pain and the heat of my own blood oozing up my ravaged thigh.

Holmes leapt forward, tossed me some distance aside with the superhuman strength Nature calls upon in emergency—the squirming beast still fastened to my burning leg—and slammed the cage door shut with the full weight of his body.

With what strength he had left, Holmes fiercely swiped Darwin's walking stick away from him and brought the hefty knob smartly down upon the red-furred beast feasting on my leg and cracked open its skull, though its jaws tenaciously clung to my flesh. Holmes continued his assault on the rodent doggedly clinging to my limb till, finally, the hellish jaws slackened, and the creature dropped with a lifeless thud. Holmes offered the stick, still dripping blood, back to Darwin. "My apologies," Holmes muttered with uncharacteristic chagrin.

Darwin and he then knelt beside me, cracking apart blood-stained fragments of plaster from my limbs. With freed hands I pulled away the last of the hellish bonds and pressed a kerchief to my wounds.

"Sherlock," Darwin declared between labored breaths, "we must stop meeting this way."

"Indeed. Sir Charles, I can hardly believe my eyes."

"I overheard all. We must destroy the beast's records, Sherlock," said Darwin. "All of them, before the world learns too soon what terrors lie in wait."

"I believe my pistol may still be of use," Darwin declared, drawing it into my hand. "With my compliments," he said.

We turned round to the rattling cage, the blackguard's form disintegrating in the hideous, contorted mass of bristling red hair. My stomach turned with the crunch of bone against gnashing teeth.

It suddenly struck Holmes to ask, "How in Heaven's name come you to be here, Sir Charles?"

"A certain young woman contacted me in an extremely distrait state of mind. She said that she could think of no one else in whom to turn. On the strength of having met me through your interview and because she feared for your safety, she pleaded for me to aid her in any way possible in keeping you from harm.

"I invited her to participate in her own mission, but she said that she dared not come near you, only handing me this note to deliver to you at an appropriate time. It seems that time is now," passing to Holmes with these words a folded sheet of foolscap which he absently pocketed.

"A remarkable story," said Holmes in a flat tone of voice, seemingly unmoved by Darwin's portrayal of Catherine de Quincey's histrionics. "Unknowingly, Sir Charles, you have just confirmed a point of interest. But, please continue."

"With resources of my own," Darwin added, "I learnt of your return on the *Matilda Briggs*. I have been dogging you ever since." And then he winked. "Some detective, Sherlock."

"I believe you have missed your calling, Sir Charles," replied Holmes. "The world lost a great detective when you chose to pursue the realm of pure science."

"Perhaps," Darwin said cheerily, "but in earnest, Sherlock, save for my Emma's happiness I give nothing in my life higher priority than the safety of England's only *consulting* private detective."

"I am deeply flattered, but truly, how on earth did you find us in such a hellish maze?"

"Remember, Mr. Sherlock Holmes, I sailed half the oceans in my youth. Along the way, Captain Fitzroy taught me many a navigational trick. And aboriginal companions in Tierra del Fuego were generous in sharing their mastery of silent tracking and stalking methods with me."

Darwin broke into a hearty laugh, adding, "Never in my wildest dreams could I have appreciated the part those humble skills should one day play." His laugh suddenly turned into a rasping cough, then Darwin clutched at his heart and turned a chalky white.

"Are you game for more adventure?" Holmes asked. His broad grin I took as a clumsy attempt to hide deepening concern for Darwin's well-being.

"Tush, a minor attack, Sherlock. I shall be fine."

"And you," Holmes directed at me, "are you up for more adventure?"

"Quite," I replied, ignoring the oozing wound to my leg. "But first, we must attend to Lucy!" With these words, Holmes nodded, even as his brows drew themselves into deep, puzzling furrows.

"Just remember, my friend," Holmes said enigmatically, "things aren't always what they seem."

We three rose unsteadily and began trudging stiffly in the direction of Hearseborne's study. Turning a corner, we suddenly came upon two roughs carrying a large silver platter between them, Hearseborne's ill-fated feast groaning with elephantine portions of steaming delicacies. The five of us froze in our tracks, staring nervously from one to the other.

"What's this 'ere, now?" one asked gruffly. "I thought I 'eard a scuffle."

"It is finished," Holmes declared solemnly.

"Is 'e done for, then?" the other thug asked, squinting leathery eyelids.

"Yes," Holmes replied flatly, whilst I waved the pistol between them. "Do you intend to give us trouble?"

A moment of tense silence passed until the first ruffian admitted, "Don't knows 'bout you," glancing at his companion, "but I'd as soon polish off this 'ere grub as get in a scuffle with these blokes."

I made a sweeping gesture for them to pass and cautiously marked their transit with my finger pressed snugly upon the revolver's trigger. We left them behind, a scene of comic horror with the blackguards splayed on the floor, noisily gorging on lobster and pheasant, obscenely smacking their lips and raucously laughing like mischievous, overgrown street arabs.

With a deep sigh of relief, I discovered Lucy Gates unharmed. I attacked the bonds and with their release, she swooned limply forward from the chair and moaned, "John, John, how you must despise me."

"Not a bit of it," I whispered in her ear, Darwin and Holmes silently looking on. "I can but imagine what vile threats impelled you to bring us here."

"Is it truly possible you could forgive me?"

"After we have left this dreadful place," I replied, "I shall spend my life proving that to you."

We warmly embraced, and then she went limp.

Suddenly, the sound of applause inexplicably echoed in the great hall, and turning round I saw Holmes clapping his hands in a measured, derisive beat.

"A brilliant performance, young woman," he declared. "Brilliant! But is it Catherine de Quincey or Lucy Gates that I address?"

"What on earth are you saying?" asked I in profound bewilderment. "And where do you see Catherine de Quincey?"

"In your arms!" declared Holmes.

"Are you mad?" I countered, looking into Lucy Gates' vivid, blue eyes.

"As I have said more than once, you look, Watson, but you do not see. Or is it the blinding force of love that hides from your sight that pear-shaped mark upon her throat?"

With a gasp, I turned my eyes to the birthmark at the base of her neck, the pear shape I had seen once before, not on her throat but on the throat of another, the throat of Catherine de Quincey the night of her rescue. With instinctive revulsion, I pushed Lucy away from me, her hands thoughtlessly gathering tatters of blouse to cover her exposed throat.

With wide-eyed incredulity, I found myself muttering, "No, this cannot be true. Why, Lucy, in heaven's name, why?"

In her silence, Holmes must have felt the need to explain further. "Snatches of truth here and there, Watson," he declared. "A relative of Charles Babbage to be sure, but also a trained, consummate actress who may don a wig, an accent and a demeanor with utter ease. I have met my match, to be sure, in the histrionic arts.

"A young woman who enjoys her jewels and her silver, enough to pit two friends against each other and to fog our minds with extraneous tensions and distractions for the sake of profit, no matter the consequences or the source. Until, for whatever reason, as Catherine de Quincey she gave the impression that she wished to come to our aid. An unforgivable act of betrayal in the eyes of Hearseborne, hence the beatings and the restraints. Is that not so, Miss Lucy de Quincey or whatever your name is!"

"Yes!" she shrieked defiantly. "And take these to hell with you." She bent forward, and two egg-cup sized half-spheres—the lenses that had transformed the warm-brown eyes of Catherine de Quincey into the cornflower blue pupils I dreamt of so many agonizing days and nights—dropped into her cupped hands, half-spheres which she violently threw in our direction.

"My God, it *is* all true!" I blurted out. "All is lost."

Sensing the sharpness of my pain, Holmes moved to my side to whisper, "She is not worthy of you, my friend."

"And what of you, Mr. Sherlock Holmes?" the young woman cried out. "Is there no one worthy of the Great Detective? I have come to this end for the sake of my feelings for you."

"Stop speaking rubbish," Holmes flatly declared. "You are no longer a threat to us. Stay here and behave, and we shall help you escape this abominable place. My friends and I have grave work to do, then we shall return. Do you understand?"

After a moment of silent pouting, she relented, saying weakly, "Yes, Holmes. I understand."

"Rest here then," he ordered, "and we shall return shortly." With strange regret I left Lucy, handed back Darwin's pistol and collected my Eley's off the floor, fitting the pistol grip snugly in the palm of my hand.

We then searched the yawning hall, bits of marble and shattered crystal crunching beneath our feet, echoes of Hearseborne's wrath. Darwin began searching massive desk drawers, whilst Holmes and I hurriedly inspected shelves groaning under leather-bound treatises.

Suddenly a shriek pierced our ears. We turned to the entrance of the study where stood the pathetic creature I had seen kicked and beaten by Hearseborne. Tears streamed down its cheeks, a wild look in its eyes and a heavy bludgeon swinging in its hand. I pointed my pistol's barrel directly at the creature's heart.

"You kill master?" it exclaimed, accusingly.

"Yes, your master is dead," Holmes declared triumphantly. "You are free now."

"Free?" the creature blankly repeated, looking back and forth between us questioningly. "You kill master!" he cried, panic building in his voice. "What I do? What I do now?"

"Do you not understand?" asked Darwin. "You are free, man. No one will hurt you again."

"We have come to destroy this awful place," I added. "All his work."

The creature's eyes widened in alarm. "The Great Work? No!"

It ran to a far corner of the heavy drape, barring it protectively with one arm and waving the heavy club in its other hand.

"Great Work. Magic from God."

Holmes cautiously neared the wild creature, the pistol in my hand cocked and ready. Calling forth his most soothing manner, Holmes said, "All is well, my good man. We wish you no harm."

With a step more of Holmes, the creature leapt forward with a violent swing of the bludgeon. Holmes just missed the force of the club's blow, parrying with a shiatsu thrust and knocking the creature to the floor. It sprang up with renewed force and swung now at Darwin, who stepped back to avoid its blow and stumbled to the ground, his revolver clattering to the floor. As the creature raised the crude weapon against Darwin again, I fired my Eley's. Its head exploded as it flew back, coughing up blood and splintering a heavy, burled side-table with the weight of its fall.

"I think," said Darwin, burying his broad head in his hands, "that I have had my share of adventure for many a day, Sherlock."

"Then rest, Sir Charles," Holmes said, "whilst I explore by that curtain." I saw Holmes feeling along fissures in the damp, slippery wall until a barely perceptible lever hit his index finger, upon which an irregularly shaped passage split off with a deep rumble from the rest of the wall.

"Sir Charles, Watson!" he excitedly exclaimed. "I believe I have found it!"

Darwin joined me as I helped to splay the stone door fully open. An evil, fetid stench immediately hit us in the face; then we noticed with horror a line of human heads hanging like gourds from the ceiling by rough cords, each grotesque trophy methodically labeled, numbered and dated, some unspeakable investigation of Hearseborne's.

The secret chamber was cramped, with a low-hanging slanted ceiling, and reeked of dank and decay. Vials, pipettes, great balloon flasks and other laboratory paraphernalia familiar and unknown to me rested on web-veiled shelving beside manuscripts stacked several feet deep. Dim, flickering gas-light did little to speed the progress of our search.

Suddenly Darwin let out a yelp of unbridled joy. In his arms he lovingly cradled two large leather-bound volumes. Hand-written labels on the spines read L and M.

"My private notes!" exclaimed Darwin, beaming.

"Excellent," Holmes declared. "We must burn all the rest. No one must know of the rest."

"Yes," Darwin concurred. "It is too dangerous."

I located a flask of solvent on the floor and splashed the volatile liquid throughout the chamber in broad swaths, then ran back to Lucy Gates and the site of the massive book, Hearseborne's crushed body underneath.

"John!" she cried with outstretched arms.

"Lucy…that is not who you are, is it? What then is your name?"

"Brigid. Brigid O'Shaughnessy."

"Up to it or not, we must get you away from here, Brigid." The name stuck in my throat.

I helped her to her feet and with her arm round my neck, we awkwardly shuffled back to Hearseborne's library. The vapours were choking now as we readied to exit.

At the doorway, half his face shot away, suddenly stood the determined little creature, a blazing sconce now in its trembling hand. "Magic go. All go!" it cried hoarsely, blood streaming down its chest. The creature lifted its arm to toss the fiery wick our way.

Holmes grabbed for the flaming torch and swung the creature round into the alcove slippery with solvent, then dove through the door as the sconce touched home. My ears popped with the blast, a blistering fire-ball ballooning out from the stone door and lapping the high ceiling with tongues of red flame.

"Darwin!" Holmes bellowed, peering into the crackling inferno.

Then we heard Darwin's faint voice behind us.

"Here, Holmes," he said weakly, his notes firmly tucked under his arm. "You must have missed me rushing out as you tackled that pathetic creature. I haven't moved so fast in many a year."

"One task more lies before us," Holmes now declared. "To ensure that the hellish beasts in their cages are consumed in this purifying conflagration."

Whilst we were in Hearseborne's secret chamber, the rats had set upon the bars of their cages with their grotesque, razor-sharp incisors. As we approached, they were still shaving away great curls of the iron rods that fell to the floor with a metallic clang. The look of their fierce, red eyes upon us as we splashed them with the last dregs of solvent seared itself forever in my mind.

I shall never forget their horrid squeals as Holmes stepped several meters back to safety, swinging a blazing lantern and catapulting it between the bars to shatter and explode in an all-consuming ball of flame before them. Even alight, crisping as we looked on with a thrill of horror, the rats pursued their desperate gnashing of the metal bars until one by one the beasts fell—little more than charred bone—to the steaming floor.

Luckily, the remainder of that evening was relatively uneventful as we wended our way back to the surface. By that time, Darwin was in a very bad way. His breathing was labored and uneven, and he had broken out in a cold sweat.

Holmes pulled me aside by my coat-sleeve to say, "As for the young woman, Watson, what are we to do with her?"

"I don't know, Holmes," I admitted. "She has injured us both, most grievously. And yet…"

"As far as I am concerned, I have better use of my time than to pursue charges against her. And perhaps your time is better spent, as well."

"Yes, I see what you mean, Holmes," I reluctantly concurred.

He then instructed me to find a cab for the woman I had known and come to love as Lucy Gates and then to accompany the great man back to his beloved Down House. Meanwhile, Holmes would remain behind to rally the river police and to help quell the fires we had ignited in the catacombs below London.

As I assisted the woman I now knew as Brigid O'Shaughnessy into her cab, the warmth of the rising sun turned cold on viewing up close the damage that had been wrought upon her, her arms and throat blotched with numerous contusions and bearing the marks of several deep cuts. Despite my outward reserve and the pain she had inflicted upon me, even then I longed to caress her as I shut the cabin door and watched her cab ride out of sight.

In the bleak, early morning light, I boarded the first train out with Darwin to Sydenham. And as I watched the great man rock to and fro soundly asleep in our cabin, I somehow knew that he would soon be lost to us.

CHAPTER 25

The Return Home

From the sitting-room, I listened to our worthy landlady answer the door and mumble greetings upon Holmes' ingress. I followed the tramp of his shoes up the familiar steps. The door swung open, and in stepped Sherlock Holmes. For the second time in our brief association, we put our arms round each other and heartily embraced.

"Holmes, you don't know how happy I am to see you safely back in our rooms," I warmly said.

"And I," he added. "It was close, very close, my friend."

We looked at each other in the manner that only two people sharing great joy or tragedy exchange a look.

Despite his uncharacteristic ebullience, Holmes appeared weary to the bone and haggard in the extreme. I suggested the recuperative powers of sleep to my friend, not even cognizant of my own injuries inflicted by the horrid rats.

Holmes said little more save to inquire after Darwin's physical condition. Frankly, I cloaked my concern; Holmes had been through enough. He moved to the window, lit a cigar and for a moment stared meditatively out at the scene below, then retired to his room, leaving me to review the swirl of events of the past twenty-four hours.

How differently I had imagined its denouement, Lucy Gates' hand in mine as we watched the glow of the sun envelope the panorama outside the window of my sitting-room. The adventure and lack of sleep would have caught up with her by then, and her beautiful, golden eyelashes would be fluttering with the call of sleep as she slipped into my arms. I would not have been able to recall a sweeter moment in my life. Alas, my reverie was shattered with the landlady's distinctive knock.

"The young lady is at the entrance," Mrs. Hudson said through the door.

"Young lady?" I echoed. "Lucy, here to see me?"

"Catherine de Quincey, Doctor. She begs to see Mr. Holmes. And at this hour, mind."

"Mr. Holmes?" I parroted again.

At that moment, Sherlock Holmes appeared with his morning pipe in hand. He moved to the window and languidly gazed outside moving not a muscle, smoky wreaths rising slowly from his nostrils. Mrs. Hudson, who had stepped inside, and I exchanged glances, wondering in unison, I guessed, what could be going through Holmes' complex mind. Then he turned his tall, gaunt frame to us and walked slowly and deliberately up to the good landlady.

The delicate fingers of his right hand slipped into the pocket of his dressing-gown and withdrew a small but distinctive slip of paper, the note from the young woman that Darwin had earlier handed him. Slowly, deliberately, he tore it in pieces and tipped them into Mrs. Hudson's palm.

"For the lady," he declared, "and say to her, 'With love.'" Sherlock Holmes walked back to his bed-room and quietly shut the door.

CHAPTER 26

A View to a Life

Holmes sat staring into the fire, the flames playing on the trim of his beloved dressing-gown, his long, sinuous fingers tapping nervously on his knees. The warm yolk-coloured glow made deep shadows of the hollows of his high cheek-bones and the sockets of his eyes.

I have heretofore failed to mention a distinctive and fascinating peculiarity of my friend's features, a quality of his eyes: One lens permanently dilated, more so in times of duress, and more brilliantly coloured than the other (a shade of slate-grey flecked with muted blue). To-night, this distinctive characteristic of Holmes appeared heightened.

He had been sitting all day in an orgy of self-recrimination and doubt, wringing his slender hands, uncharacteristically imploring me to endorse his actions. Naturally I was as comforting as I could be, my heart going out to my friend in his hour of need.

"Watson, Watson, did we the right thing?"

"Yes, given the circumstances."

"But the knowledge we destroyed, Watson. Think upon it."

"Holmes, you saw yourself the monstrous consequences—"

"—In Hearseborne's hands, Watson! His hatred for life in all its complexity clouded his mind to the creative process in evolution. Consider to what benefits a man of Darwin's dimension may have applied that incredible science and the great secrets hidden in the Akashic records, in the treatises of the Nine Unknown Men and in Mendel's papers. All that we have discovered, from the first fire to the mysteries of electrical energy, may be put to good or to evil. It was Hearseborne who twisted this leap of knowledge to perverse aims. Knowledge itself is pure, is it not?"

"Is it, Holmes?" I pondered aloud. "Perhaps man is meant to go only so far, to keep a safe distance from the inmost workings of creation."

"Rubbish!" exclaimed Holmes. "Where would we be, my good fellow, had man followed that course? If there be a purpose in life, it is for man to dig and to dig and to never stop digging till his nails be clotted with the very stuff of eternity."

I filled my pipe with another round of *Ship's* and drew in the blue flame of a match-stick into the bowl. "Perhaps a better time shall come to apply those forces Hearseborne had too early unleashed. Did he himself not acknowledge that he had not the tools to realize his horrific plans?"

"There does seem a time and a place for all things."

"Certainly," I concurred, "consider Pasteur's investigations into toxins whilst elsewhere, independently, other men worked along similar lines. It was the hour for that knowledge to be bestowed upon us, and only a higher power has that timetable. The day will come, Holmes, to make good use of those powers Hearseborne was so desperately seeking. He was truly out of step with the natural harmony of the world."

"Brilliant, though, Watson. Twisted and brilliant."

"My God, Holmes," I pondered, "how does one fall to that depth of depravity?"

"A singularly intriguing point. I must confess that I have often considered such a problem, Watson. Should I pass a group of children lost in play at Regent Park, think you I glow within with happy thoughts of their carefree time of life? Alas, my tendency is to reflect upon the evil influences already at play upon their tender lives.

"To what hidden cruelties are these children subjected within the sanctuary of their very homes? By the drunken father? By the slothful mother, abused herself by her father when she was a child? And by what other dark powers are these children daily diminished?

"It is a vexing business, my friend. And to think that this monster in human guise was once an innocent child himself."

"Perhaps his childhood was of such nightmarish proportions," I commented, "that we may never come near to imagining its horrors, Holmes."

Holmes shrugged, and a peace seemed to settle upon him. We heard a knock at the front door and the sound of Mrs. Hudson shuffling in its direction.

In a moment, our good landlady was handing Holmes a message and a small package. Upon unfolding the wire, Holmes' chin sank upon his breast.

"We have lost Darwin."

"My Lord," I said, the words coming out in a whisper, "Darwin lost. A sad day, indeed."

Holmes, unable to speak, handed me the wire which read thusly:

> Dear Mr. Holmes:
>
> Charles passed away last night. He was surrounded in the final moment by all who loved him save you, his hand in mine, and he left us peacefully.
>
> Should any thought cross your mind that the adventure which he shared with you and Dr. Watson and later recounted to me, contributed to his condition, I must assure you to the contrary. The affair had the effect of a tonic, of putting new life in his step for many a day thereafter. He seemed to me, at times, the Charles Darwin I had grown up with and had come to love so earnestly as a young girl.
>
> Our plans are to hold a simple service and to have Charles rest beside his brother, Erasmus. Lest you misunderstand, we would invite you and your companion to attend but for the publicity your appearances should certainly incite. I trust that you and the good Doctor shall respect our caution in this regard.
>
> As for the package, Charles requested that I send the item to you in grateful consideration of the time he shared with you and for all your efforts in his behalf.
>
> Rest assured that you and Dr. Watson shall forever remain in our heart and honoured guests of ours in Down House.
>
> Yours In Deepest Appreciation,
>
> Emma Darwin

I sat in numbing silence, stunned despite my presentiment of Darwin's short time left on earth.

"Kindly open the parcel," Holmes requested of me, his voice cracking.

The book, *On The Origin of Species,* lay in my trembling hands, inscribed within with these simple words:

To Sherlock Holmes, a fellow voyager in high adventure.

Yours Always,

Charles Darwin

"'Beware when the great God lets loose a thinker on this planet,'" recited Holmes to himself. I looked up to see my friend swaddling himself against the cold in our very warm sitting-room.

"Montague Street," he whispered.

"Montague Street?"

"Where I lived, Watson, when I first arrived in London, the world one degree more innocent, then," said Sherlock Holmes. "I must visit Montague Street. Alone, dear friend. And tonight."

CHAPTER 27

The Conclusion

Once past the elation of that great and terrible adventure, riddled with self-recrimination, Holmes nevertheless pursued his work with continued distinction. There were, of course, the final purges of giant Sumatran rats that had somehow escaped the great conflagration, and that required Holmes' skilled supervision—not without mishap, unfortunately—but on the whole a campaign successfully fought.

During their extermination, the occasional rat would surface in the oddest of places, victimizing a neighborhood for days until it was eventually cornered in some alley, shot and disposed of. For months, every report of a missing child threw the City into a panic and to be honest, numerous children did vanish, never to be heard of again.

Another peculiar and ferocious set of attacks seemed focused on the City's less fortunate women, concentrated most oddly in the Whitechapel area. Whispers even abounded that the three vicious slayings had been the work, not of the Sumatran rats, but of a madman on the loose. By year's end, however, with the last organized campaign to eradicate the giant rats, the assaults and the rumours they spawned appeared to stop coincidentally.

Much as Holmes and I applied ourselves to hushing reports of attacks by the Sumatran rats, with little success, we were elated that, at the very least, their association with Hearseborne's terrible discoveries and experimentation never came to light during this awful period in London's history. To this end, Holmes and I had sworn solemn oaths to each other.

All the while, what Holmes and I discovered on that hellish island by Sumatra haunted our thoughts and many a sleepless night. Holmes was determined to return with a small army of trustworthy men, tactical as well as medical and scientific, to ensure that every vestige of Hearseborne's evil work was eradicated for all time.

The year came to a bitter end. Holmes and I celebrated the Christmas season as best we could, and in the spring we renewed our campaign to obtain a well-stocked ship and capital from various sources. By mid-year, through Mycroft's not inconsiderable influence, Holmes and I had even managed an audience with Her Majesty on two occasions to discuss sponsorship of such a venture, ending both times with declarations of concern and promises of the deepest consideration but no commitment.

Then, one day in the first week of October as Holmes and I waited for Mrs. Hudson to bring up our tea, my eyes fell upon the following startling report in the afternoon edition of *The Times:*

> Volcanic Eruption—We have been favoured by Lloyd's agents at Batavia with the following particulars of a volcanic eruption at the island group known variously as Krakatau, Krakatan Island and Krakatoa:—"On the morning of August 28 a volcano in the Sundra Strait between Java and Sumatra erupted violently at approximately ten o'clock in the morning local time, destroying volcanoes known as Danan, Perbuwatan and most of Rakata.
>
> "Witnesses reported that the explosion was most horrendous, spewing great quantities of hot ash, flaming boulders and pumice debris hundreds of kilometers and generating colossal waves called 'tidal waves' 40 meters high wreaking complete devastation throughout the region. It is estimated that 50,000 or perhaps even more inhabitants in the affected area have been killed by the monstrous eruption and its ensuing effects. The bloated bodies of animals, men, women and children spill forth everywhere one looks and the threat of epidemic grows with every hour."

Holmes and I came to learn that the enormous, incoming waves loosed by the awesome explosion had made a direct hit upon the tiny, horseshoe-shaped island where so many horrors, we were certain, had been hiding: The result was utter destruction.

We argued many a time thereafter whether the hand of God had moved that day on behalf of all mankind. Holmes, of course, ever relished driving home the point that had some divine intervention occurred, His hand certainly slogged in a very, very wide and indiscriminate path.

I should not even attempt to second-guess the manner in which the Creator works his wonders. Who can name the hidden agenda behind the powerful forces at play all about us?

I remain contented that from every tragedy, whatever its cosmic purpose, some good, some strange beauty arises, as in the exotic colours and halos of the sun and moon I have witnessed of late, effects—the scientists claim—of the tons of debris spewed into the atmosphere upon Krakatau's demise.

For all the mysteries I encountered with Holmes in the singular journey recorded within these leaves, no mystery is stranger, more perverse, than love. Despite her treachery, the deep pain she inflicted upon me, for many a day and night I found myself recalling that oddly beautiful morning I found Lucy Gates sitting before me. Though I may love again, till the day that I die I shall never forget her.

I shall take Life as it comes with all its mystery and surprises. Just now Holmes has informed me of a new client approaching the doorstep. What adventure and turns-of-fate, I wonder, await us both?

About the Author

Lauren Steinhauer has always been deeply involved in the arts and a storyteller. As a young boy, he drew constantly, carting around a large sketchbook wherever he went when not entertaining friends by hypnotizing them and telling them interactive stories. Later he became absorbed with oil painting and old master techniques. His early heroes were an uneasy pairing of Norman Rockwell and Salvador Dali.

In his school days, he wrote poetry and short stories, not for assignments but as another means of self-expression. As a young man, Lauren worked at Universal Studios with Albert Whitlock, Alfred Hitchcock's special effects wizard. During this period, Lauren was also a regular performer at the world-famous Magic Castle, performing professional magic in all of the club's showrooms. He moved on to designing movie posters for major Hollywood studios and art directing campaigns for numerous agencies, studios and clients in Los Angeles, often providing ideas for slogans along with writing advertising copy.

In the early 80s, Lauren moved to San Francisco and began his career in computer graphics using the Lisa, Apple's precursor to the original Macintosh. Since then, Lauren has provided creative services for clients such as Apple Computer, Claris Corporation, Pacific Bell and Novell through his own company, Steinhauer & Associates, and through groundbreaking multimedia groups such as The HyperMedia Group and HyperPro. In the early 90s, he began his teaching career giving intense one and two-day computer workshops throughout the country and was among the first faculty members of San Francisco State University's Multimedia Studies Program. Currently, Lauren conducts graphics and multimedia courses at Laney College in Oakland, California.

In the mid-90s, Lauren wrote a series of three books for IDG, Worldwide, ending with the publication of *Macromedia Director 6 Studio for Dummies* in addition to writing *Director 6 Studio Skills* for Hayden Books. During this period, Lauren rekindled his interest in creative writing and completed *Sherlock Holmes' Lost Adventure: The True Story of the Giant Rats of Sumatra*. For a complete change of pace, Lauren recently began an ambitious and potentially controversial contemporary novel with the working title, *Hoax,* set against the lingering moral issues so deeply entwined in the Holocaust experience. While he continues to offer creative services through Steinhauer & Associates, Lauren is preparing to market Virtual3D™ enhanced video to motion picture and broadcast executives, a computer process he has developed over the last two years that adds highly effective depth to regular video.

0-595-31707-3

Printed in the United States
217444BV00001B/160/A